How We Danced While We Burned
Followed by
La Justice, OR The Cock That Crew

Two Plays
by Kenneth Bernard

How We Danced While We Burned
Followed by
La Justice, OR The Cock That Crew

Two Plays
by **Kenneth Bernard**

Introduction by Gerald Rabkin

Santa Maria
Asylum Arts
1 9 9 0

ISBN 1-878580-23-X
Library of Congress Catalogue Number 90-080159
FIRST EDITION

Cover photograph by Matthew Buresch

The author wishes to acknowledge the support he has received over
the years for his dramatic work from the following sources: the
Guggenheim and Rockefeller Foundations; the New York State
Creative Artists Public Service Program; the Trustees of Long
Island University. Most important, were it not for the many actors,
theater artists, technicians, and directors (especially John Vaccaro), who worked for little or nothing, often contributing their own
resources, these plays and others could not have been presented at
all.

This book is dedicated to all those whose courage and suffering have
gone unrecorded, and for all those who have endured the anomolies
of systems of justice.

Asylum Arts
P. O. Box 6203
Santa Maria, CA 93456

Contents

THE UNSPEAKABLE THEATRE OF KENNETH BERNARD

For over two decades, Kenneth Bernard has created a highly distinctive, disturbing theatre vision too strong for most audience's tastes. Because it pitilessly refuses facile affirmations, because its fierce ironies dance around the funeral pyre of human victimization, it is a theatre that runs defiantly against the current of American optimism and canons of good taste. No surprise, then, that the plays of Kenneth Bernard should be infrequent candidates for regional theatre production. Mainstream audiences do not want to see their faces reflected back brutishly and lacerated—albeit in a distorted mirror. Nor do most want to be forced to contemplate a blasted historical landscape in which the only constants are cruelty and thwarted desire, a post-Beckettian universe without God, justice, reason, or order.

But there is a paradox at the heart of this bleak vision: Salvation may be illusory, but, as Bernard writes in an essay on the film *Grease*, "Redemption is always only a song away." And so all of Bernard's plays offer if not a solution, a strategy: concentrate on diversionary tactics to distract the executioner, stretch your comic routine at the gallows as long as you can. Despite their core existential pessimism, Bernard's plays are, therefore, determinedly *playful*. They are the reverse of closet drama; aggressively theatrical in their use of music, dance, film, costume, color, make-up, noise, they insist that drama must transcend language to recognize the autonomous power of performance, which is not a reflection or interpretation of life, but life itself.

It is thus no surprise that Bernard's plays have been most successfully realized productionally in collaboration with a highly idiosyncratic director whose vision matched his own even as it sprang from different impulses. John Vaccaro co-founded the Play-House of the Ridiculous in the mid-sixties in response to a new sensibility born of Pop-Art and emerging gay consciousness. "We have passed beyond the Absurd," wrote the other founder and first playwright of the Ridiculous, Ronald Tavel, "Our position is absolutely preposterous." The Ridiculous responded to meta-physical preposterousness with transvestism and tacky travesty, presenting a three-ring circus of drag queens, speed freaks and would-be Superstars, a world over the brink. Consciously embracing bad taste, sexual ambiguity, phallic eroticism, and operatic flamboyance, the Ridiculous theatre abjured political attitudinizing and avant-garde pretensions. But, in the ferment of the late sixties, it shared with other experimental theatre of the era a radical dissent from middle-class values.

When, after being impressed by the Play-House of the Ridiculous' production of Charles Ludlam's *The Conquest of the Universe* in 1967, Kenneth Bernard sent a copy of his play *The Moke-Eater* to its director, John Vaccaro, he initiated one of the most fruitful collaborations in contemporary American experimental theatre, one which has survived several crises, and though suspended since 1984, will perhaps resume again. Since 1968 Vaccaro has staged the great majority of Bernard's plays: two short plays— *The Lovers* and *The Monkeys of the Organ Grinder*, and seven major plays—*The Moke-Eater* (1968), *Night Club* (1970), *The Magic Show of Dr. Ma-Gico* (1973), *The Sixty Minute Queer Show* (1977), *La Justice* (1979), *La Fin du Cirque* (1984), and *Play With An Ending* (1984)—most of them at the experimental New York venues La Mama E.T.C. and the Theatre for a New City. Since the mid-eighties, Vaccaro has increasingly withdrawn theatrically and the Play-House of the Ridiculous has ceased to function. (The mantle of the Ridiculous was passed to Charles Ludlam's Ridiculous Theatrical Company, now struggling to survive its own crisis—its leader's tragic death.) With the passing of Vaccaro's Play-House, Bernard lost his most hospitable theatrical forum, a theatre willing to abandon what Bernard rejected: what is "proper" ideologically and structurally to a play. As non-Play-House productions of Bernard's plays have revealed, Vaccaro and company offered a level of intensity and energy difficult to replicate.

Bernard's plays were the perfect dramatic vehicle for the manic style that Vaccaro had evolved. And the plays—concise, disorienting, outrageous, and fiercely ironic—helped refine that style, for Bernard was much more concerned with the dark forces that govern human experience than Ron Tavel or Charles

Ludlam. By confronting Bernard's plays, the Play-House deepened its concerns and invested its pop imagery with more disturbing resonances.

The collaboration began in 1968 with *The Moke-Eater*, a nightmare vision of *Our Town* America, a frontal assault on naïveté which can recognize neither the evil it confronts nor the evil it creates. A travelling salesman, Jack, finds himself stranded in a prototypical American small town when his car breaks down. He jauntily asks the townspeople where he can get it repaired and is welcomed with gleeful menace as someone desperately awaited named Fred, a designation Jack vehemently rejects. The townspeople turn ugly and animalistic at this denial, and led by their grimly-ironic boss, Alec, submit the hapless Jack to an escalating series of grotesque humiliations which leave him physically and psychically stripped.

With Alec as Master of Ceremonies, Jack is forced to witness or participate in a sadistic series of charades which he has no choice but to endure. Finally reduced to impotent infantilism, he will admit to anything, even that he is Fred, and is allowed to leave town; but not before he observes the Moke-Eater—the amorphous manifestation of the destructive energy of the play—devour an old man as victim. But the escape is itself a charade. The "little show" is not over: as Jack's repaired car speeds quickly away, the townspeople freeze in the precise positions they held at the beginning of the play. Jack reenters; his car has broken down again. Although he left three hours ago, he has not left, he cannot leave, he will never leave.

In Bernard's next play with the Play-House, the theme is even more ambitious than the death of American innocence: the Death of Civilization itself. *Night Club* (1970) takes place in the moment before Apocalypse. It is set in Bubi's Hide-Away, a small subterranean, windowless room in which an androgynous compère presides over a show comprised of a series of inept, desperate acts performed by members of the trapped audience: a ventriloquist unable to control his lecherous foul-mouthed dummy, a juggler who destroys expensive crockery and antiques, etc.

Bubi effusively presents the mangled performances with all the hyperbolic enthusiasm he can muster—*anything* to keep the show going. The audience on stage—clearly a surrogate for the actual audience—responds with desperate dependency. They intone Bubi's name incantorily as though it were a magic charm. Only he can save them, only he can hold back the darkness, the ominous marching, explosions, jack-hammers we hear seeping through the walls of the refuge. The Hide-Away is rotten, decaying, but it is all that remains: the Last Bunker. Bubi drops his campy hysteria from time to time and desperately, sincerely tries to communicate with someone—anyone—outside, but there is no reply.

So all he can do is escalate the desperate diversions. The show reaches a literal climax as Bubi encourages the audience to join in a mass copulation to the *Wilhelm Tell* Overture. Sex is the ultimate anodyne. A young man refuses to join the communal embrace. "The menu says there is no cover charge!" he insists. But Bubi points out "There's always a cover charge, darling, didn't you know?" and the young man is dragged screaming to the stage and beheaded on a makeshift guillotine. And as Bubi, with real love and sincerity, cajoles new "tricks, songs, dances" from his desperate charges, even the severed head of the young man responds with reciprocal ardor: "Bubi! Bubi! Bubi!"

In his next collaboration with Vaccaro, *The Magic Show of Dr. Ma-Gico* (1973), Bernard broadened his canvas to deny the balm of culture. *Dr. Ma-Gico* is set in the past, in a court suggestive of that of Louis XIV. But if Bernard's materials are courtly, romantic, fairy tale, his use of them is anything but gentle and nostalgic. The magician, Dr. Ma-Gico, for the "entertainment" of his entourage, conjures up a series of episodes that uniformly end in horror, betrayal, or disgust: a girl is torn to pieces by Gypsies who demand that she dance for them; a Prince has to decide whether a fat ugly dancer or an old slobbering King is his enchanted Princess, and makes a fatal mistake; a Queen is fucked to death by her royal consort; and, finally, Ma-Gico slits the throat of a suspicious King. Ma-Gico ironically sums up the grim proceedings: "And so justice again triumphs...and the good people of my court are entertained for a day. God is truly bountiful."

A cold, severe play no matter how assiduously Vaccaro worked to frame and distance the cruelties through courtly gavottes and stylized acting. Bernard uses his traditional materials to ferociously indict the historical ubiquity of human brutality, particularly the mendacities of those *in power*. He is fascinated, not unambiguously, by the central image of the King, the ultimate symbol of authority: on one level, political power victimizes art, but on another, the illusionist-artist plays both the King *and* his assassin. Never simplistic politically, Bernard implies that art itself is not immune from the corruptions of power.

The Sixty Minute Queer Show (which Vaccaro directed in 1977) carries forward Bernard's fascination with violence and authority. The figure of the King is central to every episode: as in *Ma-Gico*, the play climaxes with his assassination, this time as a drag queen delivers a painful monologue of personal loss. The conjoined "royal" image of brutal King and drag Queen poetically unifies a plotless "show" which presents seemingly unrelated monologues and turns. For this reason *The Queer Show* reveals most purely Bernard's dramatic esthetic: despite their thematic consistency, his plays are intended to work on a level of metaphor that resonates beyond conscious understanding. Bernard's ubiquitous Masters of Ceremony—Alec, Bubi, Ma-Gico—*try* to impose esthetic order on chaos, but their power—the artist's power—is confounded by recalcitrant reality.

The King represents order imposed from above: arbitrary, brutal, authorized, logical. The opposed image is that of the Queer, in the broadest sense of the word. Bernard accepts the gay connotation (a clear indebtedness to his theatrical collaborators) even as he moves beyond it. As the character of the Culture Queen states: "Queer is queerer than you think." Queerness challenges not only the fixity of sexual roles but the order and logic the King embodies. The marginality of queerness is not celebrated, its ostracism not condemned; queerness is one half of a persistent metaphoric dialectic between images of order and disintegration.

Which brings us at last to one of the plays contained in this volume, *La Justice* (1979). Here Bernard's perennial obsessions remain the same but are pursued through a somewhat atypical dramatic strategy. Even in the structured *Moke-Eater*, Bernard's plays are dominated by the "formless" armature of a show with its capricious sequence of acts ordered by the commanding "direction" of a demonic compère. In *La Justice*, however, the structure is based on a traditional dramatic device, the trial, which makes this Bernard's most accessible play. But though we are offered familiar representatives of litigation—judge, jury, witnesses, prosecutor, defense attorney—they do not play according to the prescribed rules. The accused may be vilified as "wholly devoid of morality and sentience," but he/she (?) never makes an appearance. Nor is the "vile" crime ever specified. As the Judge's wife demands: *"What is the crime? What is the crime?"*

What indeed? As the play progresses it becomes increasingly clear that a horrific crime *will* be revealed, even though it will not be committed until the play's end. And the perpetrator? No less than the dispenser of justice himself, the King of the courtroom, the Judge. *La Justice* moves on two interwoven trajectories: the trial proper and the Judge's domestic world. The former increasingly fragments as the attorneys spout arcane legalese and the jury becomes ever more irrationally mob-like and hysterical (no celebrator of the heroic masses, Bernard); at home, the Judge is propelled toward violent retribution—on his own children. ("I am a judge! I *judge*!") Bernard specifies that the set of the play conjoin the two realms, that the courtroom contain the Judge's bedroom and dining room. As the public realm dissolves into rhetorical obfuscation, the private realm ascends with tragic inevitability to a bloody, *Medea*-like climax. Because of Bernard's customary determination to work through violent imagistic juxtapositions rather than a logical unfolding of argument, the thematic implications of his play are multi-levelled. No doubt, however, that the possibility of *any* principle of justice, social or metaphysical, is skeptically interrogated. (For a persuasive analysis of the play's thematic sub-text read the author's lucid notes on the play also included in this volume. But the very nature of his consciously postmodern esthetic welcomes variant interpretations.)

One of the most problematic images in the play—and in some of Bernard's other work—is the figure of the only witness who, in his second-act appearance, enters as an ornate but "musty drag queen," a disguise which thinly masks what he *really* is: a middle-aged stock Jew. In his first turn he displays all the most offensive linguistic and behavioral traits of gross anti-Semitic stereotype; he is a comic, an entertainer, a whiner, a money lender, even a chicken flucker. (In similar stereotypic fashion, in *Night Club*, the owner of Bubi's Hide-Away, Baron Pincus Rothschild, cries sleazily, "I am going broke... Bubi, you are killing one good Jew kid.")

That the stereotype is evoked with high irony should be abundantly clear from the cumulative imagery of *La Justice*. Bernard explicitly states in his stage directions that the Jew should be seen as "striking out from beneath the stereotype." Indeed, his reemergence as drag-queen water commissioner reinforces Bernard's familiar metaphoric dialectic between King and Queer. If the Judge is the authoritarian King, the Jew is the marginalized Queer who recognizes that he cannot expect justice and must distract and placate his auditors in order to disrupt proceedings which may well convert him from witness to victim. He indeed succeeds in partially winning the volatile jury ("Jew ... we're with you."), though aware that at any moment they can turn against him viciously. The water commissioner-drag queen ploy is another desperate diversion, and he responds to the penetration of his disguise with gross aggression, finally moving beyond irony to deliver a summative jeremiad against universal decay: "I tell you the pipes are corroded. They are clogged. If they do not burst, it will all back up . . . . It will fill all your houses, your institutions . . . Nothing is clean but the shit itself!"

The irony should be obvious, but abundant evidence exists from Swift's *Modest Proposal* to the Wooster Group's *Route 1 & 9* that the higher the irony the sharper the double-edged sword. Bernard himself has recognized that the power of performance lies in its ability to convey the immediacy of life; but this immediacy has the power to overwhelm the dispassion necessary to an acceptance of the ironic. Indeed, one crucial flaw in Vaccaro's otherwise brilliant production of *La Justice* was the inability of the actor who played the Jew to find the means to convey Bernard's essential point that "he was not the stock Jew but rather the Jew *playing* the stock Jew for his own deep reasons." (Bernard's notes, p. 132) When images are as visceral as they are in Bernard's plays they inevitably inhibit his ironic intentions. Vaccaro had in fact cut one sequence in *Night Club*—a ferocious send-up of racism which, however, used gross black stereotypes—because he realized that in the racial climate of 1970 it would be misunderstood.

Bernard's audacious esthetic makes the unspeakable practices and unnatural acts in his plays hover on the brink of intolerability. Though individual thresholds of toleration vary, he has written one play so painful in its ironies that it has never received a major production: *How We Danced While We Burned*, the other play in this volume, was too strong even for Vaccaro and debuted at Antioch College, Ohio, in 1973 where it was adjudged by its student reviewer "a very strange play." An attempt was made to present it soon after in New York City, but Bernard himself canceled the production because it failed to project his intended ironic outrage, without which, he realized, it could be grossly offensive.

The play is particularly difficult to produce because Bernard focuses his familiar violent strategies on the most painful event in contemporary history: the Holocaust. In Bernard's other plays individual representations of cruelty are always distanced by a non-realistic, trans- or ahistoric frame; despite their theatrical concreteness, they are metaphorical barbarities rather than documented fact. Not that *How We Danced* is a realistic play: it is set in a symbolic cabaret with the décor of a German beer hall which consciously breaks the frame of the proscenium. The entire theatre space is the cabaret; tables are jammed together, and there are tiered benches around the walls where the audience and performers intermix. Panels behind the patrons slide open periodically to reveal watching guards. Within this hellish, fetid space a play is enacted whose main strategies are very much those of *Night Club*. A demonic compère presides over a series of pathetic acts by desperate participants. But in this show the social roles of compère and performers are historically specific: he is the Commandant and they are inmates of a death camp. Whereas all of *Night Club*'s performers do not suffer an immediate fate, here all acts end via the play's central scenic image—a heavy metal door above which the sign EXIT marks the gateway to extermination.

We know this Hell was more than metaphoric, that camp inmates were conscripted into orchestras and boxing competitions by their culture and sports-loving annihilators. So when the Commandant, like Bubi, charms, cajoles, encourages, grossly banters with his pathetic performers (who here have dehumanizing numbers rather than names) it is impossible to find any humor in his conscious, sadistic performance. Without the palliation of comedy, Bernard's anthology of horrors in *How We Danced* (e.g., "Waiters wheel in a man on a serving table. He is nude and trussed like a pig with an apple in his mouth.") indeed seems unbearable. Which like Claude Lanzmann's interminable litanies of victimization in *Shoah* is precisely the point. Bernard knows he is playing a dangerous theatrical game, but he refuses to sanitize the unspeakable. His play's governing metaphor arises consciously out of the play's epigraph: Jean-François Steiner's observation that "Treblinka has become a theatre, the ring a stage, the prisoners spectators." As the prisoner-performers are called from the audience—hence underscoring our universal vulnerability—they respond to their final command performances differently: some strive to ingratiate, placate, seduce, humiliate themselves to delay their fate; others are sullen or defiant, some even attempt to revolt. All disappear under the EXIT sign. There is no escape, nor any heroic death as in the *Chanson de Roland*, which is presented as a Christmas play. The frenetic, hallucinatory world of *How We Danced* is overwhelmed by silence—the silence of God and the silence of the rest of the world. The audience is complicitous; it watches.

It is this explicit spirit of moral outrage which, for me at least, renders tolerable the play's brutalities. Another Steiner, George, claimed in *Language and Silence* that the Holocaust renders all art insufficient. Bernard does not disagree and counterpoints not only vulgarities but sublime art to his cruelties: No higher irony is possible than the line in Schubert's *Frühlingsglaube*, sung by a visiting celebrity, that "Die Welt wird schöner jedem Tag. [The world becomes more beautiful with every day.]" And Bernard ends his play with music from Bach's "Actus Tragicus" Cantata No. 106 over the Commandant's fading voice. If an attempt at representing the unrepresentable is made, Bernard implies, it cannot accept art's formal consolations; it has no choice but to risk its receptors' revulsion.

More than the gross cruelty of its imagery, *How We Danced* is deeply disturbing in its conclusion, a scene which seems to blur the distinction between killers and victims. For most of the piece the Commandant has represented the sadistic Other, the demonic instrument of arbitrary annihilation; but in the play's powerful climax he delivers a revelatory monologue which reveals his own victimization. He screams out that he "paid for his job" with the destruction of his own wife and children. Like his own victims, he "*got instructions.*" He assumed the role of Commandant to avoid being killed himself: "Hang myself? . . . *Commandant does not hang himself! Commandant gives orders! Orders!*"

This is troubling because on the surface it appears to accept the murderers' rationale that they acted out of compulsion, obeying orders in order to survive. Again, Bernard's penchant for complex ironies and metaphoric strategies has got him into trouble by suggesting a thematic position he in fact rejects. Though this is a play soaked in the indelible blood of history, it cannot be read only on the level of historical allegory; as in all of Bernard's work, particularly *La Justice*, it challenges the metaphysical possibilities of justice and rational order. The Commandant's compulsion to "give orders" echoes the Judge's compulsion to "judge." Each process is built on power that must self-destruct because it is built on the sand of lies and hypocrisy; rational, just order is an impossible ideal. And so, on a metaphysical level, victim and victimizer *are* conflated—both are puppets manipulated by cosmic indifference, randomness, irrationality.

But there are crimes and crimes, and Bernard does not deny the guilt of murderers. Indeed, the violence of his art can be seen as an attempt to bestow esthetically a justice which human society cannot provide. His outrageous plays demand that we refuse to forget human brutality, but to make us remember, Bernard will not work conventionally; he will derange our expectations. Thus, in *How We Danced*, he audaciously widens the figure of the Commandant to subsume his very victims. The opening directions instruct the actor who plays the Commandant to speak "with a heavy Jewish accent." That this is more than a gesture of humiliating mockery is revealed by the controversial final monologue in which the Commandant assumes the role of historic witness *to his own crimes.* "The world is silent," he shouts in English *and* Yiddish. His last child, whose death he movingly recounts from the point of view of the pursued, is named Itzik, a Jewish name. The horror, the horror—"Somebody, he's got to live to tell about it," says the Commandant. This intensely felt moral burden is indeed the antithesis of exculpation.

Space precludes extended discussion of Bernard's other plays—whether directed by Vaccaro (*La Fin du Cirque, Play With An Ending*, both 1984) or by others (*King Humpy*, 1975; *The*

Panel, 1984). Suffice to say that each pursues aspects of the themes we have discussed through Bernard's customary strategies: *King Humpy* centers on the archetypally "queer" figure of a scorned hunchback; the other plays amplify the familiar metaphor of the show (extended to film and television) to record art's pathetic but determined attempt to transcend meaninglessness and brutality.

It is this faith in the dogged persistence of art, however insufficient, which prevents Bernard's plays from falling into nihilism. If uncompromisingly bleak, Bernard's theatre is not despairing. As the playwright himself wrote in a note appended to the program of the Atlanta production of *Night Club*: "If there is any hope at all for mankind, it lies in honesty and recognition of reality, particularly the unreconstructed and unreconstructible nature of the human creature. Man, I would hope, endures *in spite of*. His dignity, courage, and beauty do (sometimes) triumph sufficiently over the grossness of finitude to lift our spirits. It is my wish that plays like *Night Club* encourage, even demand, such honesty and recognition, even while they 'entertain' (and I do insist on that)."

—Gerald Rabkin

How We Danced
While We Burned

"... Treblinka has become a theater,
the ring a stage, the prisoners spectators."

Jean-François Steiner, *Treblinka*

Photo by Matthew Buresch

How We Danced While We Burned was premiered at the Antioch College Workshop Theatre on December 3, 1973. The play was directed by Beverly Grant Conrad., with music direction by Brad Brickman, costumes by Joy Conley, Sound by Dennis Gillanders, Films by Tony Conrad and Jud Yalkut, Set Design by B.Conrad.

Musicians for the first performance:

Sandy Baringer; Carla Sabloff; Hugh Kerr; Oliver Veling; Jonathan Bergen

Cast:

The Commandant	Patricia Arlin
Guards	Peter Menis; Matthew Buresch
Waitress	Lynn Collins
# 47	Daniel Brock
# 89	Jaguar Marcus III
#124	Marc Bluestein
# 22	Daniel Brock
# 29	Sheldon Horowitz
Little Girl	Wendy Weiner
Little Boy	Devon Susholtz
Doctor	Holly Miller
Patient	Lynn Collins
Hitler	Daniel Brock
Goering	Spencer F. Pinney
Himmler	Richard Pell
Eichman	Larry Pacheco Esq.
Patrons	Marc Bluestein; Nathalie Paven; Elizabeth Lucke; Spencer F. Pinney; Anne Mendelsohn; Dale Brown
Dancers	Kate Ruben; Adele L. Talarico
# 52	Sheldon Horowitz
Gerta Von Stahlhausen	Daniel Brock
# 107	Wendy Weiner
# 108	Devon Susholtz
# 109	Sheldon Horowitz
# 16	R. Nikki Todd
# 3	Devon Susholtz
# 41	Constantina Stanislaski
# 300	Wendy Weiner
# 11	Peter Menis
# 12	Matthew Buresch
# 200	Wendy Weiner
# 207	Steven Lane
# 289; Kalman Loeb	Spencer Rex Davis
Prisoners	Steven Lane; Sheldon Horowitz; Daniel Brock
The Voice	Bill Patterson
New Commandant	R. Nikki Todd

CHARACTERS

COMMANDANT (also CHARLEMAGNE)
MUSICIANS
HITLER and ENTOURAGE
GERTA VON STAHLHAUSEN
DOCTOR
GUARDS
WAITERS and WAITRESSES, from whom
      ROLAND
      OLIVER
      ARCHBISHOP TURPIN
      KING MARSILE
      CHRISTIANS and PAGANS
PATRONS and PRISONERS, from whom, in particular,
      PUPPETEER
      DWARF
      BELLY DANCER

How We Danced
While We Burned

This play takes place in Hell. The decor is that of a small, overheated German beer hall. The front wall is velvet red. Except for a space up front, tables jammed together. Tiered benches around the walls, from which people conducted to the tables when vacated. Sliding panels around theater, except for front wall, through which men look in periodically. Exactly in the middle of the velvet wall, a heavy door over which the sign EXIT. The proprietor of the beer hall is called the COMMANDANT. He wears an ersatz uniform and affects the military manner, e.g. saluting, clicking his heels, bits of marching drill. He speaks English with a heavy Jewish accent, sometimes German (fake or real), and smatterings of Russian, Polish, Hungarian, etc. (also fake or real). Bows obsequiously to audience from time to time. As the play opens (very unobtrusively), patrons, waiters, waitresses (attractive) serving and eating and drinking, which continues throughout the play. Beer hall music. Movement. Maybe dancing. Cast and audience mixed, and dressed the same. The waiters and waitresses have a proprietary, even condescending, air towards the patrons. Sometimes they laugh shrilly in their faces or fondle them with blood-curdling endearments in English, Yiddish, German, etc. They also whisper things (e.g. about them) in the COMMANDANT's ear in passing. Eventually the COMMANDANT struts out and tries, unsuccessfully at first, to get the crowd's attention. Backtalk where possible.

COMMANDANT: Hey. . . Hey, listen to me, you bums. . . [*To* MUSICIANS] Give me an introduction. [*A clumsy introduction from the Yiddish musical theater. Patrons still inattentive. He shrugs, then does a short tap dance, followed by a fanfare*] Hey!. . . Hey, what I gotta do, show you my cock-a-doodle-doo?

VOICE: Yah, show us your cock-a-doodle-doo.

COMMANDANT: [*Searching*] I left it home. [*Scattered laughter*] My wife's got it. [*More laughter*] She won't leave the bed! [*Everyone with him now*] You

23

got it every day, she says, give me a break. It's grounds for divorce, don't
you think so?

VOICE: You got a replacement?

COMMANDANT: [*Searching again*] So! You want to get personal now? Have
I got a replacement? What kind of a guy you think I am, huh? You got a
replacement yourself, buddy boy? Huh? You're a fresh kid. What's your
number? [*Laughter*] —Listen, now I got your undivided attention finally,
let me introduce— [*He runs several feet off, marches back to music, turns
smartly, salutes*]—Commandant! your host and owner of this clip-joint.
[*Shrugging*] —Listen, I gotta make a living, too.

[*Scattered phony cheers, etc.*]

VOICES: *Achtung! Achtung! . . .*

[*Groans, etc., during following speech*]

COMMANDANT: Yah, you got it right for once. Attention is the word. We got
to get the rules right first thing. We got a lot of rules, all kinds of rules,
you wouldn't believe it till you heard it, and you got to obey the rules here.
Like we don't dirty up the floor. Yah, that's right. We don't dirty up the
floor here. No pigs. We got a clean place. You understand? All right. So
here's a few rules already. First and foremost, when your number's called,
you gotta come up, no matter who you are. No shrinking tulips and
daffodils allowed. And when you come up, you gotta do your own thing,
three-four minutes, maybe you gotta chance even. But if you flop, you
gotta go, no question. You ain't even got a prayer, understand? Thumbs
down and you go [*Pointing to the EXIT*] out, O-U-T, that's it, you're a has-
been, a nobody. Like in the words of the great philosopher, it's a great life
if it don't kill you first. [*A few laughs*] That's first and foremost. All the rest
is second. Like no spitting, no screaming, no smooching, no crybaby stuff.
And no crapping in your pants. Remember, we don't dirty up the floor. We
ain't no reform school here. You see somebody throwing up you hang a
bucket on his face. We got a first class operation here and nobody leaves
a mess. You should take it personal, like a reflection on your character.
Then—no hiding any money, no letters, no temper tantrums, no monkey-
ing around and horseplaying, no heart attacks, no heartburn, no
speeches, no religious service—we got everything you need—no bird calls,
no disgracing your parents and other relatives. Eat, but not too much,

everybody here is a lady and a gentleman. No sleeping, no telephone calls, no having children—it's not allowed, absolutely—no medicine, no cough drops, no picnic lunches, no secrets, no new clothes, no gambling, no squeezing pimples or blackheads, no shampoos or haircuts, no playing with yourselves—that's a hard one, I know from experience—no rough stuff, no snootiness or snottiness, no pets of any kind, no books, games, or puzzles, no talk about the good old days, no suicides, no primping with mirrors, no making faces, and no harmonizing, there's maybe a few more later, if you don't object, please.

[*Silence*]

VOICE: How about swallowing?

COMMANDANT: Swallowing all right but be quiet about it. Same thing breathing.
[*A few mock cheers*]
Okay. So now we got business. We're late already. Big shots back there, they don't come on time. But we take care of them, huh? Just remember your number. [*Table thumping*] Yah, we take care of them. So is everybody ready for the big klonk in his life?
[*Groans*]
What? You're not ready? Okay, just to show you how reasonable I am I'm providing you a quick diversion. [*He does a thirty second fancy marching drill, complete with commands and audience participation*] All right, so there, I'm a regular bleeding heart. Now you got no complaint. Right?
[*More groans*]

VOICES: More!
          Encore!
          Don't stop! . . .

COMMANDANT: You can't get enough of me, huh? Oi, they should only see me in Warsaw. —But I'm strictly a dancer type. I can't vocalize for two cents. [*Coins thrown out. Singing badly*] "I'm singing in the rain . . ." You see what I mean? It's the dry climate. I belong in Miami.
[*Cheers*]

VOICES: Pepsi-cola!
          Hot dog!
          White House!

Betty Grable!
George Washington!
Want to fuck, baby?
Brooklyn Bridge!
Cocktail!

COMMANDANT: Oi, they would love me in Miami Beach. But the union wouldn't allow it. Besides, [*Shrugging*] who's got the time?
    [*Groans*]
—No, no bellyaching! Remember the rules. We are keeping business separate from pleasure. Right? You want to get me in trouble? [*He reaches into a bowl*] Okay, so number forty-seven already. Forty-seven, where you are? You got a lucky number. We're gonna take suspense right out of your life.
    [*#47 comes up*]
You got a number, mister? Can you do the tango or a cha-cha-cha? Swallow your tongue, maybe, shoot a bow and arrow?
    [*#47 holds up two hand puppets*]
Hoi-hoi-hoi, we are starting with a professional tonight. Fancy, fancy.

> [*The* COMMANDANT *signals, and two waiters bring out a chair and puppet stage. #47 sits behind the stage and holds up the two puppets,* PUNCHINELLA *and* ROSCOE. *His face is visible throughout. During his act, which is strained and clumsy, the patrons voice disapproval, e.g. "Throw the bum out," "Extinguish him," "Give him to the soap machine," "Oi, get rid of him." They also comment on the puppet play, laugh, imitate the puppets, etc.*]

Okay, so give us the business already.

PUNCHINELLA: Roscoe! Roscoe! Where are you?

ROSCOE: I'm right here. Are you blind, Punchinella?

PUNCHINELLA: Maybe I am. I didn't see you. Where were you last night?

ROSCOE: Last night?

PUNCHINELLA: Yes, last night. Stop playing for time and answer the question.

ROSCOE: I forgot the question. Would you repeat it?

PUNCHINELLA: *The question is where were you last night.*

ROSCOE: Where were *you* last night?

PUNCHINELLA: Why do you have to know *that*? A much better question would be *whom* was I *with* last night. [*She laughs*]

ROSCOE: All right, *whom* was you *with* last night?

PUNCHINELLA: Wouldn't you like to know!

ROSCOE: [*Hitting her*] Listen, *libechen*, if you've been cheating on me—

PUNCHINELLA: Oh! Oh! You're a beast and I won't tell you.

ROSCOE: [*Laughing*] Who would want to sleep with you?

PUNCHINELLA: Well, you would. For one. You *do*.

ROSCOE: Not any more, if *I* have anything to say about it.

PUNCHINELLA: —Roscoe, I'm pregnant.

ROSCOE: You mean—

PUNCHINELLA: Yes! We're going to have a baby, a little Roscoe!

ROSCOE: [*Clutching his heart*] Ah! Ah! [*He sings*]

> Punchinella, I adore you,
> Punchinella, you are sweet,
> Punchinella, you're adorable,
> Punchinella, you are—

[*He can't find the word. Patrons shout possibilities. The* WAITERS *kick down the stage and drag him towards the EXIT*]

ROSCOE: Wait! Wait, I'm not finished. Wait!

[*They push him through. Only the arm with* PUNCHINELLA *sticks out*]

PUNCHINELLA: Roscoe! Save me! Roscoe . . . Our baby! . . . [*They hammer her head and push her in. She screams. The door is shut*]

VOICE: [*Imitating*] Roscoe! Roscoe! Save me!

[*Laughter*]

COMMANDANT: Roscoe's a bum, too.

[*Laughter. With several* WAITERS *and* WAITRESSES *he dances and sings*]

COMMANDANT, ETC.:   Ve klonk der Jews on der head,
Ve spritz mit gas till dey dead,
Den ve burn dem up in der oven
For Jews ve ain't got no lovin'.

COMMANDANT: Okay, so that's number one for tonight. We did a bang up start and I'm proud of you. But we gotta keep moving. Remember, *reputation*. Dogs we are not having any in this show. —And a good speed. Like racers in a hundred yard dash. Schoo! —Oi, what a fast runner.
    [*Groans*]
No, no! We gotta keep it moving. The railroads are coming in like rabbits on us. We are swamped right over our heads. [*Filtering the numbers in the bowl through his fingers*] Look at them! How we gonna keep up with them? Huh? You got a solution, number eighty-nine?

[*A young woman rushes up giggling. Cheers, kissing sounds, whistles, comments. A Brooklyn accent*]

#89: Oh, Commandant, I'm so thrilled.

COMMANDANT: You got more thrills coming, baby. You better believe that.

#89: [*Coyly*] Are you any part of them, Commandant?

COMMANDANT: [*Going into a fag act*] Me? Oi, have you got the wrong party. [*He mugs and winks at the audience. Laughter*]

#89: I think you're so cute, Commandant.

COMMANDANT: You think I got a cock, dolink?

#89: How could you not?

COMMANDANT: Well, it's a very long story, let me tell you.

#89: I really go for you, Commandant.

COMMANDANT: Yah. But where you gonna go, dolly? You got a number, maybe?

#89: Only for you, Commandant.

COMMANDANT: So let's have it!

> [*He snaps his fingers.* #89 *does a strip while marching and reciting. The* COMMANDANT *sometimes interpolates and joins in, but still in his fag act. Her stripping is awkward. She trips, she falls, she rips clothes, she becomes frenetic and desperate*]

#89: [*Marching and stripping*]
Commandant, Commandant
I love the Commandant.
Commandant, Commandant
I love the Commandant.

COMMANDANT: [*e.g. fluttering, wiping his brow*] Oi!

#89:   I love him in the morning,
I love him noon and night,
My love to him is calling,
I love him all my might.

COMMANDANT: [*Marching a bit*] Oi, what a dilemma, let me tell you! That one's the Miami two-step.

> [*Cheers, whistles*]

#89: [*With patrons joining*]

Commandant, Commandant,
I love the Commandant.
Commandant, Commandant
I love the Commandant. . .

[*Stripped, or nearly so, disheveled, and rubbing against the* COMMANDANT]
Oh Commandant, let's make music.

COMMANDANT: You got any professional training?

#89: Try me.

COMMANDANT: Dolly, I only play the harmonica.

#89: Play mine.

COMMANDANT: Oi, what an imagination! You must be a Litvak.

#89: We could play to beat the band.

COMMANDANT: Hmm, that's got possibilities, you know. Where are them boys, anyway?

#89: [*Frightened*] Commandant! I'm young and I'm beautiful!

COMMANDANT: It's a matter of opinion, dolly.

#89: Take me! It's all I've got!

COMMANDANT: [*Touching her vulgarly*] Oi, and what a bushel.

#89: Let me make love to you!

COMMANDANT: In this heat? Dolink, you need a rest.

#89: [*Screaming*] I'm not tired!

COMMANDANT: Dolink, I said you need a rest! —Boys, give a hand, please.

[*Several* WAITERS *lift her over their heads*]

#89: [*Struggling*] No! No! Leave me alone! I'm too young! I'm a virgin! You prick! Oh, you goddamn prick! . . .

COMMANDANT: Oi, what a misnomer. —You're surprised I got such a vocabulary, huh?

> [*Whistles, cheers. The* WAITERS *throw her through the door as she screams*]

COMMANDANT: What a hot number, huh?
> [*Silence*]

Hot, you get it? [*Tepid laughter. He marches briefly, imitating*]

> Commandant, Commandant,
> I love the Commandant.

Oi, what a hot number, I'm telling you. Here's another hot number, I'm gonna bet you—number . . . one hundred twenty-four. Who's the lucky boychik?
> [*An old man with a suitcase walks up*]
What do you know, a grandpoppa. Hey, grandpoppa, how old are you?
> [#124 *spits at him*]
What a nasty temper. Tsk, tsk, in such an old man such a temper. You ain't worried about blood pressure, a heart attack? You got a tap dance, maybe?
> [#124 *spits again*]
What's in your suitcase? Come on, show me.

#124: No!

> [*They struggle over it, it opens, it is full of old dolls*]

COMMANDANT: Ahhh, you got a family, I see.
> [*The old man tries to pick them up. The* COMMANDANT *kicks them out of reach, laughing*]
They ain't gonna get away, old man. I got them, every one.
> [*The old man, suddenly broken, cries, then begins to rock and chant*]
Hey, cut that out! No holidays here. No crybaby stuff.

> [*The* WAITERS *rush up, grab him, and move him roughly to the EXIT*]

Wait! Wait a minute, boys! Bring over here the old geezer. So! A smart Alec,
huh? A wise guy?
> [*He slaps the old man in the face, then takes him in his arms*]
> [*To* MUSCIANS] Boys! [*Tango music. They dance. The old man breaks loose
> and turns to the audience*]

#124: Yiden! . . . [*Laughing through his tears*] Yiden! . . . Yiden! . . .

COMMANDANT: Hey, get rid of this nutcracker old man. Send him back to
Israel. He's a lousy dancer, anyway.

> [*One or two laughs from patrons, both cut short. The door is
> slammed shut*]

#124: [*Muffled*] Yiden! . . . Yiden! . . .

COMMANDANT: A crazy. A crazy one. That's how it goes sometime. One day
it's all crazy ones, another day nice like lambs.

VOICE: Baaa!

COMMANDANT: Good! Good! A sense of humor, that's what I like. What good
is living without a sense of humor. [*He chants briefly the religious tune of
the old man*] —And I like music with a little lift to it. Give me a cue, boys.
> [*He sings a song from the Yiddish musical theater, e.g.* "A Yiddish
> maidel darf a Yiddishin Boy." WAITERS *and* WAITRESSES *dance and
> chorus with him*]
Now, ain't that more like it? Listen, I got a funny story I'll tell you. —But
wait, let me get one more number cooking for the time being. Give me a "t."

PATRONS: [*Shouting*] "T!"

COMMANDANT: Give me a "wenty."

PATRONS: "Wenty!"

COMMANDANT: Give me a "nine."

PATRONS: "Nine!"

COMMANDANT: And what have I got?

PATRONS: Twenty-nine!

COMMANDANT: I got a twenty-nine out there?
                    [*A woman and three children come up. They walk
                    straight to the EXIT, heads down*]
Now that's a cute one. Four for the price of one. Look at that. I speak about
lambs and right up they come. Your eye falls on a bargain, you pick it up,
right? —Hey, wait a minute. Too fast, too fast. Whoa.
                    [*He gives the children Halloween masks, lollypops,
                    balloons, and noise-makers. One of the children tries to
                    frighten him with his mask, then gives him a flower*]
Oi, this kid, he's touching me right where it hurts. They don't bring them
up like this no more. What do you say, huh?

CHILDREN: Thank you.

        [*Whistles, cheers, table pounding*]

COMMANDANT: Okay. Now off you go with your mommy, huh? [*To mother*]
Here, have a towel, sweetheart. Giddyup.

        [*The woman opens the door. Noise-makers*]

CHILD: Is Daddy here?

MOTHER: Yes. He's over there. On the other side.

CHILD: [*As door is shut*] Daddy! Daddy! . . . Daddy!

        [*Sound of balloons popping*]

COMMANDANT, ETC. [*Immediately*]

                    Ve klonk der Jews on der head,
                    Ve spritz mit gas till dey dead,
                    Den ve burn dem up in der oven,
                    For Jews ve ain't got no lovin'.

COMMANDANT: [*Tossing the flower behind him*] Hoi-hoi-hoi! You want to
hear a good one? Boy, have I got a story? Don't you believe it? Listen, I
don't lie. Not in hard times like this. Just read the newspaper, you'll see
what I mean. And those dopies in the other camp, they're planning to

escape. Yah. They're planning to *escape.* So where they gonna escape? In the *cooker? [Laughter]* A whole organization they got. Rabbis even. You know what their trouble is? —They don't work hard enough. Too much time on their hands. And too many questions. When is a scratch a lump? Who can answer such questions? With a gun in their head they're asking when is a scratch a lump and what day of the week is it? It makes a difference? Bah. *Porters* they are. Traffic managers. A little baggage here, put the shoes there, sometimes a bump on the head with a shovel if they're too slow, poking with the fingers you know where. Now tell me, you call that work? Pulling teeth, *that's* work. *Digging.* Dragging deadbeats in, out, in, out—*that's* work. And look at the heat—like a furnace, day and night. We got a smell would kill fresh air. And they're gonna escape. Listen, they even got time to choke themselves a little. Can you imagine it? You finish a day's work, and then you set yourself up with a nice little choke. Just because they got your *number?* Listen, everybody's got your number. So where's the choke? From such people you get *escape?* I'll believe it when I see it. And for you, forget it. You got better things. —Like how about some musical chairs? —Number thirty-six, number thirty-seven, number seventy-five, number seventy-nine, number ninety-one, number six. And any volunteers. *Snell! Snell!*

> [*Seven people trot forward, male and female. The* WAITERS *set up five chairs*]

Now listen everybody for the music. Remember Rubenstein, Godowsky, Gabrilowitch. Show everybody how you got some beat.

> [*Music, e.g. a freilach, a waltze, a hora. They walk around the chairs*]

Skip a little. . . . Now hands on your heads. . . . Behind you, like you're skating. . . . *Yah, yah,* now hop like rabbits. Come on, everybody a bunny rabbit. Hop, hop, there's a real good bunny rabbit. Wiggle the noses. Look at that. . . . We crawl! . . . Fast! Faster! . . . Now ducks! Everybody ducks, with quacking. Come on, quack, quack. . . . I liked the bunny rabbits better.

> [*The music stops. For a moment they do not realize it. Then a mad scramble for the chairs. Pulling, pushing, fighting, cursing—a free for all, until they are exhausted. One chair is broken*]

Okay, kids. Stop! That's it. It was a good fight, and the best ones won. Right? [*He shrugs to the audience*] It's right if you say so, right?

> [*Four are seated, three are on the floor*]

Congratulations. Now, all you bunny rabbits in the chairs, quick, hop into the rest rooms, wash up and look pretty, right over through there.

> [*He points to the EXIT. Looks of horror, fright, dismay. The*

WAITERS *herd them in. They are too tired to resist*]
No, no, no. No complaining about the management. It's a corporation
anyway. Nobody you know personal. Just give a hop and a skip and a jump
like the four little rabbits. Without your breath it's gonna be quick. You
heard of the little tailor who got seven in one blow? I'm not so good. I only
got four. [*He laughs. To the survivors*] But it's not so bad, huh? Come on,
my little rabbits, it's okay, you can laugh. [*Weak laughs*] Yah. You're the
little rabbits that got away, huh? You know about Peter Rabbit? He got
away in the briar patch. The fox didn't get him. Huh? Lucky little rabbits.
Go sit. What, you got a heart attack? [*He laughs*] Have a snack. Relax. So
maybe later we do another musical special number. Huh? Right now, all
we got is—umm, number . . . oi, the suspense is killing you, huh? —
Number twenty-two. Yah, number twenty-two. Where's the little rabbit
with the twenty-two?
     [*Number Twenty-two is a thin, frightened man*]
So what you got? A bargain, maybe? Nylon stockings, some olive oil,
coffee?
     [*#22 is too frightened to speak*]
What kind of number you got?

#22: [*Stuttering*] T-t-t-twenty-two.

     [*Screams of laughter. He smiles awkwardly*]

COMMANDANT: What? You're a joker? [*#22 shakes his head firmly*] Tap-
dancer? [*He shakes his head again*] Magic tricks? [*Again*] But you got
some number, right? [*He nods firmly*] So do it already, I'm a busy man, oi
am I busy.

     [*#22 begins with difficulty, grows increasingly passionate with
     fear, finishes trembling and on the verge of collapse*]

#22: Hasn't a Jew got eyes? No hands, and all the rest? Hasn't a Jew got
passion, don't he eat, don't he get sick like everybody? And children that
he loves, a wife, a family? Stick him with a spear and he's dead, tickle him
and he's laughing. When it's cold, don't he shiver? And when it's hot, don't
he sweat? And he gets sick like everybody.
     [*Bronx cheers and thumbs down from the patrons*]
He got blood, he bleeds, he got suffering like everybody else!
     [*The* WAITERS *start dragging him off at a signal from the*
     COMMANDANT]

If you pluck out his eye, he's gonna be angry! He's gonna pluck out *your* eye!

COMMANDANT: Oi, you got no talent and besides you make threats? You got a big nerve, you, a ham. [*To audience*] Vaudeville is dead, and it's a shame, let me tell you.

#22: He's gonna get revenge! He's gonna get *even*! He's got blood, like *everybody*, like *you*! You don't burn him up!
        [*As they push him through the EXIT*]
It's William Shakespeare! It's poetry! Great English poetry! Wait! You don't understand! He's got blood! It's William Shakespeare!
        [*The door is shut on him. He shrieks out a few moments*]
Shakespeare! . . . Shakespeare! . . . Revolt! . . .

COMMANDANT: Boy, what a no-goodnik type. I know about types like that. You give an inch, they take two, three, four feet even. With them you gotta be firm, a tight fist. No crybaby stuff. Listen, you want to see a good act, I made it myself? [*He puts on a huge claw and sits*] Super criminal, the claw. [*Laughter*]

VOICE: Santa Claw! . . .

COMMANDANT: Yah, I'm the Claw. They can't get me, see? Cause I'm too smart. Deep down in the sewer, I got a kingdom. Special tunnels I can go anywhere. They wind all over. Men I got working for me. I give an order, presto they do it—or else. You get me? —*Or else.* [*He laughs*] Yah. It's that *or else* that gets them. They do what I say or they are crapping in their pants with fear. The Claw don't show no privilege for mistakes or failures. Ain't that right, number fifty-two? [*A momentary confusion*] *Fifty-two! Number fifty-two!* Where are you? [#52 *comes forward*] Ahh, there you are. You got a report for me, fifty-two? [#52 *shrugs*] Remember *or else.* — Listen, you people, there's only one man I got worry about. He's a specialist in crime-fighting. Arch-enemies we are. But so far he don't get me. I'm too smart for him. I got tunnels he don't even know about. Techno-Man, he calls himself. Wherever they got machines, that's where he can be. You got a screw, presto, there he is. Hah! But down here, we don't have no machines. Right, number fifty-two? [#52 *nods eagerly*] Good, good. Rats, we got. Candles. Cockroaches, spiders, bats. Lizards even. Garbage—some of it not so bad, you can have it cheap. And the *Claw.* [*He laughs*] Tunnels everywhere! Tunnels inside tunnels! Under them even. Fifty-two, did you kill Techno-Man like I told you? [#52 *hesitates, then nods eagerly*] Then where are his fingers? Huh? —You fool! *Goyisher kop!* Dummy! You think you can deceive the Claw? *Where are his fingers?* [#52 *offers his own*] Bah! I don't want your fingers. I got them already. You *failed*, number fifty-two, you *failed!* [#52 *gets on his knees and pleads mutely*] No! No mercy for deadbeats and bunglers! Curses, I am foiled again by Techno-Man. I must go deeper in my tunnels so he don't find me. And you, number fifty-two, you know the penalty that awaits for failures. Yah! The EXIT door! That's the one.

#52: No! No! No!

COMMANDANT: Yah! Were you followed?

#52: No! No!

COMMANDANT: You were. I can feel it. You have jeopardized my unholy war against mankind and civilization. You must pay the supreme penalty.

#52: No! No, master, no!

COMMANDANT: Yah! Yah! I am foiled and you must pay penalty. [*Aside*] Crocodiles, I got there, and snakes, and big time scorpions with stingers so long. Poison frogs even. Vampires. Crazy rats. I got everything. [*To* #52] *Snell, snell!* [#52 *holds out his arms in supplication. The* COMMANDANT *rises, holds forward his claw, and advances on him*] All right, all right. You want then the *Claw.* You want the *Claw* should rip you to pieces?

#52: [*Backing towards the EXIT*] No! No! Not the Claw! Anything but the Claw!

COMMANDANT: The Claw is coming! *Is coming the Claw!* COMING IS THE CLAW!

#52: [*Entering the EXIT*] Nooo! [*He screams*]

COMMANDANT: [*Turning to the patrons*] Pretty good, huh? Laugh a little. [*They laugh*] Give me a hand, clap a little. [*Applause*] The Claw don't make no mistakes. [*Demonic laugh*]

[*Pounding from without*]

What? We got a guest, I think. An inspection maybe.
[*Soldiers march in, line up. Ballet music.* HITLER, *followed by his entourage, dances in on his toes. He wears a white tu-tu. The entourage throw flower petals as he dances*]
[*Kissing him lavishly where he can*] Ahhh, Führer. So nice of you to come. You are so beautiful. I love you. The whole world loves you. I kiss your cock. [HITLER *points to his backside*] Ah, yes, yes, I kiss your ass, too. Ahh! Ahh! You are so round and strong. I am faint with the honor you bestow on me.

HITLER: Rest!

COMMANDANT: What? What do you ask, Führer?

HITLER: Rest!

COMMANDANT: Ah! Yes, at once! I am resting at once!
[*He falls on the floor*]

HITLER: [*An impassioned speech*] I love the flowers. Each day, when my official duties are finished, I go to my flowers. I have red flowers, blue flowers, yellow flowers, green flowers, pink flowers, orange flowers, chartreuse flowers, purple flowers . . . beige flowers, brown flowers, white flowers . . . black flowers. And I love each one of them. I touch them. I fondle them. I tickle them. I smell them. I roll on them. I talk to them. I sing to them. [*A tuneless note*] —Every day I do this thing. Because I love flowers. And I got lots of them. I got more flowers than anybody. Every day I can't wait for my official duties to be over with Fifty thousand to the front! Airplanes! Cruisers! Bombs! Kill the Jews! I sign everything! —But all the time I am thinking only of my flowers. Blue ones, red ones. . . . Oh, I got everything! I got scarlet ones even. Speckled, like bird eggs. I got ten different yellow ones—amber, canary, blond yellow, you should only see them. All day I work, I do my official duties. I review the troops, I make speeches. Kill the Jews. I sign papers. Kill even the Poles and the Gypsies. You don't know how busy I am. But always I am thinking of the flowers. The flowers keep me going. Blood red, I got, even velvet. Cherry color. Who do you know got velvet? huh? *Me,* that's who! And what smells I got. All day I think of the smell, my nose can't wait. I'm like peeing all over Eva already. But when comes five o'clock, I stop everything. So kill the rest of them, too, I don't work overtime, you understand! Goering, Himmler, Eichman, all those other ones [*If they are among the entourage, they bow.*

One of them shows "dirty" pictures of piles of bodies, etc.], gluttons for their work, they're not human, they got no other side to them. But me, I got my flowers, thank God. Flowers! Yes, flowers! Smell! Smell! [*He picks up the flower that #29's child gave to the* COMMANDANT] Smell! [*Music. He dances out, the entourage and soldiers dancing after him*] Blue ones ... red ones ... purple ... green ones ... brown ... spotted ones ... Kelly green ... flamingo! ...

COMMANDANT: What a doll, huh? He should only know how hard we are all trying. Deadlines we got. Quotas. Logistics. Labor trouble. Then that gang from the other side. A tunnel they're digging. And where? I'll tell you where. Here, that's where. We got a monopoly on tunnels. Be ready, they say. Be ready for what? Where we gonna go? Israel? [*Pointing to the EXIT*] *Israel?* Brooklyn would be better. But, oi, what a transportation problem. You got any ideas, number sixteen? Huh?
    [*A middle-aged man walks up*]
Bulgarian. He looks Bulgarian. Who wants to make a bet? Bulgarian.

PATRONS: Arab!
                  African!
                  Norwegian!
                  Panamanian!
                  Eskimo!
                  Chinese!
                  Cantaloupe!
                  Count Dreckela!

COMMANDANT: No, no. You're all wrong. I know a Bulgarian when I smell one. Don't keep us in suspense, number sixteen. Give us a little Bulgarian. You want me to be wrong?

> [*#16 is a summary of the stereotypical Jew: he rubs his hands and nose, he looks shifty and greedy, he is hunched over, he has a long pocketbook secreted in the folds of his clothes, he glances around with cunning, etc. He speaks with a thick Jewish accent*]

#16: I'm not what you think I am. [*A high-pitched giggle*]

COMMANDANT: You're in disguise? You are Chiang Kai-shek maybe? Someone we can reckon with?

#16: Ummm, could be, could be, maybe. —Actually, I'm a capitalist. I'm an Aryan capitalist.

COMMANDANT: So drop your pants, we'll settle the matter quick.

#16: I got money in the bank.

COMMANDANT: Ah.

#16: I got property. Stocks, bonds, mutual funds, a restaurant.

COMMANDANT: Ah, what kind of restaurant?

#16: Knockwurst. A knockwurst restaurant. Only knockwurst and bread.

COMMANDANT: Bread? What kind of bread?

#16: Rye, what else?

COMMANDANT: Ahh! So! Rye, you have.

#16: [*Shrugging*] A concession. Sometimes, but only sometimes, a kugel—

VOICE: Kigel!

#16: —a knish, a kasha knish. Business. You know, business.

COMMANDANT: So you're not a Bulgarian?

#16: Eh. So maybe I could be a Bulgarian. What's in it for me?

COMMANDANT: A knish, maybe?

#16: So? Who am I to turn down a knish?

COMMANDANT: You got an act, maybe?

#16: I got a Jewish imitation.

COMMANDANT: Good. A capitalist Aryan doing a Jewish imitation.

[Catcalls, etc., throughout]

#16: *[Singing]*   Oi, voi-voi-voi-voi-voi-voi.
                      Oi, voi-voi-voi-voi-voi-voi.

     [Reciting]   God, what for you're giving me such a hard time?
                      I got a wife, five daughters, and a mother-in-law.
                      I deserve all this?

     [Singing]   Oi, voi-voi-voi-voi-voi-voi.
                      Oi, voi-voi-voi-voi-voi-voi.

     [Reciting]   Listen, I try to be a good Jew.
                      I keep the Sabbeth and follow your Laws.
                      But sometimes you're just too much.

     [Singing]   Oi, voi-voi-voi-voi-voi-voi.
                      Oi, voi-voi-voi-voi-voi-voi.

     [Reciting]   I'm breaking my back here for you.
                      Even my horse don't work so hard.
                      For me it never rains but it pours.

     [Singing]   Oi, voi-voi-voi-voi-voi-voi.
                      Oi, voi-voi-voi-voi-voi-voi.

     [Reciting]   So I'm fed up. My wife is a nag,
                      My daughters are ugly, and my mother-in-law is sick.
                      Put on top of that I got no money to speak of.

     [Singing]   Oi, voi-voi-voi-voi-voi-voi.
                      Oi, voi-voi-voi-voi-voi-voi.

     [Reciting]   Where do I get the strength to go on?
                      You're not going to answer me, God?
                      Okay, but remember, I'll be speaking to you again.

     [Singing]   Oi, voi-voi-voi-voi-voi-voi.
                      Oi, voi-voi-voi-voi-voi-voi.

PATRONS: Boo!
          Throw the bum out!
          Throw the bum *in*! . . .

COMMANDANT: You know, I could use a guy with talent like you. Can you wear an apron?

#16: [*Shrugging*] What's a Bulgarian without an apron?

[*He puts on an apron and becomes a waiter*]

COMMANDANT: [*Singing*] Oi, voi-voi-voi-voi-voi-voi. Didn't I say Bulgarian? From Vilna! [*He laughs*] Ahh, sometimes I get a laugh. Not often, but sometimes. It's getting harder. You understand? Let's see, now, we got three numbers together, like triplets— one hundred seven, eight, and nine.
          [*Three Hassidic Jews jump up immediately*]
Ah, the three little rabbis from Chnipichok. Did you know they burned the synagogue in Chnipichok. Yah, and they made them dance around it naked, like devils. Oi, what's the world coming to? What you gonna do for us, Boys?

[*The three Hassidic Jews sing and dance a rousing paeon of joy to God. At the end, as they are dancing backward single file into the EXIT, each is hit on the head with a hammer*]

COMMANDANT, ETC.   Ve klonk der Jews on der head,
                          Ve spritz mit gas till dey dead,
                          Den ve burn dem up in der oven,
                          For Jews ve ain't got no lovin'.

COMMANDANT: You gotta admire faith when you see it right? —Quick, number twenty-seven!

[*WAITERS wheel in a man on a serving table. He is nude and trussed like a pig with an apple in his mouth. The EXIT door is opened to receive him. Loud pounding without interrupts. Soldiers, followed by a doctor in surgical cap and gown*]

DOCTOR: Halt! Bring that specimen back!

[*The* COMMANDANT *shrinks back. He is afraid of the* DOCTOR]

SOLDIER: [*Holding up thermometer*] Yah!

DOCTOR: Thermometer in rectum!

SOLDIER: [*Sticking the thermometer in #27's rectum*] Yah! Thermometer in rectum.

[*Groan from #27*]

DOCTOR: Needle number one!

SOLDIER: [*Handing the needle to the* DOCTOR] Yah! Needle number one.

DOCTOR: [*Sticking needle #1 in*] Needle number two!

[*Gagged screams from #27*]

SOLDIER: [*Handing #2*] Yah! Needle number two.

DOCTOR: [*Sticking #2 in*] Needle number three!

SOLDIER: Yah! Needle number three.

[*The* DOCTOR *sticks in #3*]

DOCTOR: Now. Temperature.

[*The* SOLDIER *takes out the thermometer and wipes it gingerly*]

SOLDIER: Temperature one hundred eight.

DOCTOR: Bah! No good! [*Waving #27 away*] Out! Out!

[*#27 wheeled through EXIT*]

DOCTOR: [*Pinching the* COMMANDANT's *face*] Hello, dolly, you're getting fat, huh?

[*He marches out quickly with the soldiers, looking over the audience sharply*]

COMMANDANT: [*With an obscene gesture*] Oi, that was a close shave, huh? From that I need a drink. [*He gulps down a drink and rubs his backside*] Some day I'm gonna get his number.

VOICE: Hah!

COMMANDANT: —We take a break here and do a rehearsal from our Christmas show, okay? [*Silence*] Hey! I said *okay*?
        [*Cheers, whistles, clapping. The* WAITERS *dress on stage for the following roles*]
Song of Roland, huh? We don't know. Maybe we do Siegfried instead. Scene is the famous pass at Roncevaux. The rear end guard of Charlemagne's army. You all know Charlemagne? He got a favorite soldier named Roland. No, don't laugh, you got a dirty mind. Now Roland, he's too strong and brave for his own good. Betrayed by the evil Ganelon, Roland, his faithful friend Oliver, the courageous Archbishop Turpin, and their men are exhausted from fighting off the pagan Saracens under the leadership of their evil King, Marsile. He don't know it, this king, but later his hand it's gonna be chopped off, so he's gloating too soon. Anyway, one more charge and Roland and his whole bunch probably gonna be wiped out, finished. They're all gonna be killed. Oliver, who's a little smarter than Roland but not quite so noble, he's already a dying man. His breaths are numbered, that's right, numbered. And Roland, he's beside himself with deep anguish. So up he speaks to everybody:

ROLAND: Barons of France, because of me you die;
                I can't protect you, I cannot keep you safe:
                Look now to God who never failed a trust.

COMMANDANT: He's got a point but he's still got a nerve. Why wasn't he religious before, huh? Meanwhile, Oliver got the whole picture in a nutshell.

OLIVER: Roland, you are to blame.
                There is no madness in courage for good cause,
                But men should listen to reason, not blind pride.
                You were too reckless, and so these Franks have died.
                Never again will we serve Charlemagne.

COMMANDANT: *Reckless*, you hear? He's got Roland's number. I'm gonna blow my horn right away, says Roland. Don't worry about anything. Charlemagne, he'll come on the double, for me—triple even. But no, says Oliver.

OLIVER: Three times I asked, and you would not agree;
You still can do it, but not with my consent.
To sound the horn denies your valor now.
And both your arms are red with blood of foes!

COMMANDANT: He's a smart guy, Oliver, like I said. Since they're all practically dead now, what's the difference? Roland, he's gonna save himself when all the others are dead? How's that gonna look for the family? Roland he gets the general idea.

ROLAND: Oliver, brother, I'll not break my faith with you.
I'll die of grief, if not by pagan spears.

COMMANDANT: And everybody cheers—everybody left, which ain't much. Roland may be stubborn, but he's a brave guy. I'm giving him credit. He takes out his trusty sword, Durendal, it's got a name even, they're a crazy bunch, and chops off pagan heads like a crazy maniac till he's all bloody in the mouth. *Then*, I want you should listen, *then*, Roland blows his horn cause he knows he's gonna be dead in no time flat.
    [ROLAND *blows his horn*]
All around him he's got dead bodies. The Archbishop, he's got his guts hanging down. Oliver, he's way out of trouble now. And Roland, who's taking a long time, lies down finally and makes a speech. In actual fact, he makes two or three, but we got time only for one.

ROLAND: O my true Father, O Thou who never lied,
Thou who delivered Lazarus from the grave,
Who rescued Daniel out of the lion's den,
Keep now my soul from every evil safe,
Forgive the sins that I have done in life.

COMMANDANT: So what sins? Huh? How many sins can a young boy like that have? Then an angel comes special and takes his soul to Paradise. Charlemagne and everybody cry, as is natural under the circumstances. Then the sun stands still so he can catch up with the Pagan soldiers. Ganelon, he's ripped into pieces, which serves him right. Christianity, you should bless it, is saved for another day. And Charlemagne, who's got a long white beard at this time, finds Roland's body and says:

CHARLEMAGNE (COMMANDANT):

> [*In his usual accent*]
> Roland, my friend, may God forgive your sins!
> Never on earth was there a knight like you
> To fight great battles in triumph to the end.
> From this time forth my honor will decline.

> [*Cheers, applause. Costumes discarded*]

COMMANDANT: That's as far as we got. We got some finishing touches. Like maybe we'll invent a romantic interest. He's a good boy, but he spends too much time with his horse and his sword. The horse got a name, too. So come around Christmas, if you got the time, and see the show. All right? Numbers fifty-three, fifty-four, fifty-five, fifty-six, quick, get moving. No pagans allowed in here.
> [*Two men, two women get up, try to sing, dance, juggle, etc., but are pushed without ceremony through the EXIT*]
We gotta make up for that rest. They're probably no good anyway. We'll give the next fella a chance. Who's number three?
> [*A dwarf gets up*]
So stand up. What are you, a pigmy, maybe, forgive me I should hurt your feelings.
> [*#3 walks up*]
A pigmy from Pinsk?
> [*Laughs*]
Listen. Over there, they made the break. They're gonna be dropping in. Oi, what a surprise they got coming. So, pigmy, what you gonna do us for?

#3: I do impersonations. I need a dress.

COMMANDANT: So get him a dress.

> [The waiters drag up a screaming and struggling girl—e.g. "I'm not in your fucking show!"—strip her and throw her through the EXIT]
Hey, what's her number? Ach, never mind. We'll fix up the record.

[#3 puts on the dress, makes up grotesquely from her pocket-book, walks up and down seductively, mugging at the audience]

#3: Play it again, Sammy.... Hey, Commandant, I'm a living doll, don't you think? [Referring to the dress, e.g.] Lord & Taylor. —I vant to be alone! ...
COMMANDANT: Dolly, you got me wondering. Can it be you are so gorgeous?

#3: I am Goering's mistress.

[Hilarious laughter]

COMMANDANT: I believe it! I believe it!

#3: I am the toast of the Third Reich. Every soldier hangs my picture in his locker. You don't believe me? —That man over there, he don't believe me, Commandant. Oi, mein gott, what fools these mortals be.

COMMANDANT: I'll squash any fly lays a hand on you, dolly.

#3: [To man in the audience] Listen, Liebchen, we gonna meet again some day, so watch your manners. You're gonna be the laundry soap and I'm gonna be in the lady's toilette. Oi, what a wash we'll make!

[Hysterical laughter]

I got a smell like a whole bunch of roses. [Lifting dress] You want to smell, dolink? When I go down the street, even the dogs follow me. I got big blondies, they commit suicide when I don't give them my love.

COMMANDANT: Oi, I'm falling in love again!

#3: You bet your pants are are. You're crazy if you don't. Listen, bubele, tonight we're gonna make music like a whole symphony, you and me. We're gonna make a whole wedding and honeymoon. Don't you want to marry me, sweetheart?

COMMANDANT: Oi, how could I refuse a dolink like you?

#3: But don't expect no blushing bride. I'm gonna let you see my whole thing and knock you for a double loop. You ain't never seen such equipment like mine. Oi, baby, I got everything. [A few bumps and grinds] You ain't gonna believe it. It'll be the shock of your life. You're gonna be in paradise like you never been since you was a baby cradled in your mama's arms. [He sashays off a few steps] Believe me, I know what I'm talking about. [Imitating the marching of the commandant] Quick, number two million thirty-nine! Snell, snell!

[Hilarious laughter]

COMMANDANT: [Broken up with his laughing] I like it, I like it! Put on an apron, dolly. We gonna keep you around a while. A few laughs we gotta have, believe me.
[Distant pounding]
Oi, they're still going, those dummies. They think it's gonna be better for them out there? How you gonna be so dumb? Everything's like a big funnel from one corner to the other. Everybody's sliding, and here's where they gonna end up. Only down here we got a mirror for everybody's soul. You gotta end and begin right down here, in the cellar, you know what I mean? Everybody else is either a crybaby or a dope or maybe even he's dead already.
[More immediate knocking. Two guards open the door and let in a mature, very fashionably dressed, woman. Evening clothes and heavy make-up]
[Greeting her] Dolink, dolink, you ain't forgot us! [Holding her hand, to patrons] We got a special break today, you should appreciate the honor.

#3: Oi, am I appreciating.

COMMANDANT: One of the best singers in the whole world—let me present you, she's a beautiful lady, I know what I'm talking about—Fraulein Gerta Von Stahlhausen!
[*Cheers, whistles*]
She's gonna sing us a few numbers like she's done before, you should only be lucky enough to remember her last visit. But first we gotta make up for the time we gonna lose. Number two hundred eighty-nine, number two hundred, one hundred eighty-eight, two hundred seven. . . .

[*As they stand up,* WAITERS *rush them quickly through the EXIT. Some protest and resist. One, a dignified, well-dressed gentleman, breaks loose a few moments*]

PROFESSOR: [*Clicking his heels and presenting his card*] Sir, Herr Doctor Professor Schmeissen, University of Heidelberg, Oriental Antiquities and Languages.

COMMANDANT: [*Pushing him roughly*] Get out of here, you bum. You want I should ask you about your bowel movements? You think you're somebody special? Get rid of him!

PROFESSOR: [*As he is dragged off*] Sir! Sir! My card! Seven books! You are making a most serious mistake! I don't belong here! —I am *German*!
          [*They shut the door*]
German! . . .

COMMANDANT: [*To* GERTA] You gotta forgive these interruptions. Business gotta go on, you know how it is? Me, I never finished high school. [*She smiles and bows her head*] How you been, huh? You're looking terrific.

GERTA: Very well, thank you.

COMMANDANT: You been traveling around?

GERTA: Yes. I've been to the Russian front. Magnificent. The war progresses.

COMMANDANT: And have you sung again for you know who?

GERTA: Yes. Two times. He is a great lover of music. Once—yes, once—we sang . . . *together*.

COMMANDANT: Oi, what an honor. He's a great lover of flowers, too, you should know.

GERTA: Ah, I did not know that. But I am not surprised. I shall bring him some the next time I sing for him.

COMMANDANT: And don't forget to tell him who told you about it, huh?
          [*They laugh conspiratorially*]
Listen, what you gonna sing for us?

GERTA: Well, first I thought some Schubert—
COMMANDANT: Ach, I love Schubert. He is so romantic.

GERTA: And then, a new song hit that everybody in the bomb shelters is humming.

[WAITERS *hand out music, lyrics, and translations*]

COMMANDANT: Good, good, we like to keep up. Music!

> [GERTA *sings. Some whistles, barking, howling. A few people are obviously moved.*]

GERTA: [*Dubbed or not*]

> Frühlingsglaube (Schubert)
>
> Die linden Lüfte sind erwacht,
> Sie säuseln und weben Tag und Nacht,
> Sie schaffen an allen Enden.
> O frischer Duft, O neuer Klang,
> Nun, armes Herze, sei nicht bang,
> Nun muss sich alles, alles wenden.
> Die Welt wird schöner jedem Tag,
> Man weiss nicht, was noch werden mag,
> Das Blühen will nicht enden.
> Es blüht das fernste tiefste Tal;
> Nun, armes Herz, ver giss der Qual,
> Nun muss sich alles, alles wenden.

[*Applause*]

COMMANDANT: Beautiful. That guy got a soul all right. Go right through with the next number, Gerta. We know how busy you are.

[GERTA *sings the following song, in German; very sentimental*]

GERTA: My heart is with the boys at the front,
          Braving Russia's chill and fading memories.
          But in my heart I keep the spring time shining,
          In my heart there is such pining.

          For there is one among them all,
          Handsome, brave, and tall.

Come home, my blue-eyed lover
Before love's leaves do fall.

My heart is trudging through the snow;
It follows where the soldiers go;
Heedless of the wind and cold
It seeks its lover to enfold.

For there is one among them all,
Handsome, brave, and tall;
Come back, my blue-eyed lover
Before love's leaves do fall.

[*Applause, cheers*]

COMMANDANT: Oi, what a beauty. So poignant. Lucky we got heat or I'd be shivering. And maybe based a little bit on truth, hmm?

[GERTA *smiles demurely*]

GERTA: I must go now. Duty calls.

[*Groans of disappointment*]

COMMANDANT: What a pity, you gorgeous lady. You come and bring beauty to our lives, and then, like a butterfly in autumn, fly away into the fading sun.

GERTA: Why, Commandant, you are a poet.

[*The* COMMANDANT *clicks his heels and bows.* GERTA *swings her cape around her and leaves briskly*]

GERTA: Good luck to you all. Keep up the good work.

[*Cheers, whistles*]

COMMANDANT: Boy, she got a lot of impact, that girl. And class. How old do you think she is?

PATRONS:　　　Forty!

> Thirty-nine!
> Fifty!
> Sixteen!
> Two thousand!

COMMANDANT: And still a virgin. A regular Brunhilde. But what sex appeal, huh?

> [*Laughter, jeers*]

Oi, what an ungrateful crowd. Why do we bother to be so nice, I don't know. Anyway, it don't matter. We gotta make up because time is money. Right? Any volunteers? Not even a Gypsy? ... A Jehovah Witness, maybe?

> [*A few laughs*]

Too bad. I was gonna give a break. But now you're making me mad. So okay! Over here, number three hundred, over here number eleven, twelve, over here forty-one. We gonna have a contest. A talent contest.

> [*Three men and a fat woman come up*]

So you, what's your number?

#300: I sing.

COMMANDANT: All right. Couple musicians here. [*To* #11, 12] What's your specialty, boys?

#11: We box.

COMMANDANT: Couple pair boxing gloves here on the double. [*To* #41] And you, sweetheart?

#41: I'm a dancer.

COMMANDANT: A dancer? Well, it takes all types. Couple musicians here. Don't worry, darling, I ain't so fussy as you think. —Now, everybody ready? Yah? Okay, get set, and *go*, number three hundred!

> [#300 *begins singing a folk song, e.g. "Oif'n Pripechuk," in Yiddish*]

Number eleven, twelve!

> [#11, 12 *begin boxing*]

Number forty-one! —she should have two numbers.

[#41 *does a belly dance to Near Eastern music. The patrons are divided in their attention. Yells of encouragement to favorites. As the* COMMANDANT *points to each performer, his partisans cheer and applaud. He does this several times. The* BOXERS *maneuver to knock down the folk singer several times, but although dazed he gets up and sings. They try it with the* BELLY DANCER, *but she slaps them nearly unconscious. At the height of the competition, the wall to one side is broken in and prisoners from the other camp burst in. A sudden silence*]

PATRON: Kalman! Kalman Loeb!

PRISONER: [*Without moving*] Mama?

COMMANDANT: Oi! What a mistake you fellas are making! And spoiling the show besides!

[*He blows a whistle. Guards rush in, and with the* WAITERS *and* WAITRESSES *they beat the patrons and prisoners to the* COMMANDANT's *orders. Lights begin to fade slowly*]

Okay. So we got to hurry up. We wasn't expecting you so soon. You didn't know when you had it so good. Now we got to hurry it up. [*To patrons*] Get up! All of you! Take off your clothes and out. [*He points to the EXIT*] OUT!

[*The patrons are at first slow, but soon move quickly under the blows. Whatever audience is mixed in with them get out of the way as best they can. The three acts pick up where they left off until they, too, are driven through the EXIT. A few try desperately and shamelessly to make love*]

Oi, what a waste of talent. —Now, quick, you new ones, you dummies, dress up in those clothes. And don't be fussy. You got a dress, put it on. You're gonna be born all over again. Quick! Quick! We got a late show to do! We gotta keep the wheels of progress rolling. We got customers, take a look if you like. Inspections. If you hurry we got a cartoon later, maybe.
[*In the midst of these changes, the* COMMANDANT *screams out, and everyone freezes. Lights down. A spot*]

Wait! Wait! One thing I forgot [*Pause. Softly, to audience*] The whole world is silent. You hear it? [*In Yiddish*] The world is silent! [*Angrily*] Listen, you don't make no accusation, huh? What I do for you, you swine, it ain't easy. Somebody, he's got to live to tell about it. —Why me? Why not? I paid for my job. Listen, I *paid*. My wife: dead. My children: dead. The last one, Itzik, he sees me when he gets off the train. *You listen!* Me, I don't have this job then. I'm carrying the clothes they take off, keeping my head down, running. You get a black eye [*He draws a finger across his throat*] —finished. *No marks on the face, see!* And you run, you die running, you don't look, you're scared all the time.

[*Sound track of confused people, shouts of guards, train noises*] And he says, "Daddy, I've found you!" And he cries. Itzik *cries*. My little boy cries because he's frightened and he's found his Daddy. And me, I'm stopping my running. *He's my son!* My head, it's going to be smashed in. "Itzik, go wash," I say. "We'll talk later." No, no, he says, he don't want to leave me again. He's gonna lose me, he says. He's afraid. His mother— He's all alone. *My Itzik is all alone!* What's happening? he asks me. Tell me, Daddy. And me, I'm not running. I'm keeping my head low in the bundle of clothes. Itzik! I scream, for God's sake, *wash first, talk later!* — And I run, I run, I run. [*He picks up one of #124's dolls. Crying*] I run all day. All day, and still I can't sleep. He was a good boy. He went and he washed. And when he washed, when they spritzed him with . . . did he yell out—*Daddy, where are you?* I hear him! I hear him! God, I hear him! *Daddy!* —I paid! I paid! I paid! [*Wiping his eyes*] And you, you swine got a few instructions to follow. You hear? *You got instructions!* —Hang myself? Like the others who let their Itziks go wash alone? [*Shrieking, throwing down doll*] Commandant does not hang himself! Commandant gives orders! Commandant gives orders! Orders! Orders!

[*The previous activities resume. Lights continue to fade, except behind the velvet wall. Commandant's voice fades also. #3, the dwarf, stands on a chair and echoes many of the* COMMANDANT's *instructions*]

Number one: You take out your ticket. Your stub, it's got a number. Memorize it. Everybody got a number. Come up when your number's called. If you lost your stub, you're nobody, you don't exist, you gotta go right away. Likewise if you're even number over a hundred or pink in the upper left hand corner. The rest of you write down on the back skilled labor or not, what languages you speak, and how much you weigh and your height. Tomorrow maybe we change it around. Children, forget about. Women over twenty-five don't bother. Take your clothes off right away and get down on your hands and knees for personal inspection. You

got a wedding ring hidden somewhere special you get your head hit with
a shovel. We don't have no modesty here. Everybody is people like everybody else. You are gorgeous we are maybe putting you through screwing
machine. It don't hurt after first hundred times [*He laughs*] But you get
pregnant you are kaput. . . . You got any sickness, you gotta go. You got
a cough, kill it quick like a bunny or you got big trouble. . . .

> [*Lights out. Music: the bass aria, "Heute, heute," from Bach's*
> Cantata No. 106 *("Actus Tragicus"), over* COMMANDANT's *fading
> voice. Dim lights. No bows. The new "patrons" turn in their seats
> and watch the audience leave. If possible, steam sounds, perhaps
> a few whisps of smoke from floor, maybe windows in floor beneath
> which nude writhing bodies*]

END

Schubert's "Fruhilingsblaube" (Uhland)

The gentle breezes are awakened,
They rustle and float day and night,
They are everywhere at work.
O fresh fragrance, O new sounds,
Now, poor heart, be not anxious,
Now, everything, everything must change.

The world becomes more beautiful with every day,
No one knows what yet may be,
The blossoming will not come to an end.
The farthest, deepest valley is in bloom;
Now, poor heart, forget the torment,
Now, everything, everything must change.

"Oif'n Pripechuk" (On the Oven)

On the oven burns a little flame
And it's hot in the room.

And the rebe teaches the little children
The alphabet.
And the rebe teaches the little children
The alphabet.

> Listen closely, children,
> Remember, dear ones,
> What you are learning here,
> Say it once again and then repeat again,
> Komets alef O,
> Say it once again and then repeat again
> Kometz alef O.

Study, children, with great will
That is my request,

Which one of you will learn to read Hebrew
Will get a flag.
Which one of you will learn to read Hebrew
Will get a flag.

> Listen closely children . . . .

When you children will grow older
You'll understand yourselves,

How many tears lie in these letters
And how much weeping,
How many tears lie in these letters
And how much weeping

> Listen closely children . . . .

La Justice

or

THE COCK THAT CREW

Photo by Michael McKenzie

La Justice premiered at the Theater for the New City on October 18, 1979. The play was directed by John Vaccaro, with music by John Braden, costumes by Bernard Roth, masks, props and scenery by Wes Cronk, and movement by June Ekman.

Musicians for the first performance:

Dan Block	Reeds
David Nieske	Percussion
John Braden	Piano

Cast:

Court Attendant	John Barilla
Judge	Donald Arrington
Prosecutor	Joe Pichette
Defense	Geoffrey Carey
Assistants	Nasseer El-Kadi
	Kevin Bradigan
Witness	Michael Arian
Nadia	Madeleine le Roux
Son	Bart Gardy
Daughter	Barbara Goldman
Jury:	Marie Antoinette
	Kevin Bradigan
	Maria Duval
	Nasseer El-Kadi
	Chris Kapp
	Cookie Mueller
	Sally Reymond
	Rene Ricard
	Mink Stole
	Shannon Sullivan
	John Byron Thomas
	Molly Thompson
	Jerome Turner

CHARACTERS

THE JUDGE (Klaus)
HIS WIFE (Nadia)
HIS DAUGHTER (Ilke)
HIS SON
THE WITNESS (The Jew, The Donkey, The Water Commissioner)
PROSECUTOR
DEFENSE
THEIR ASSISTANTS
THE JURY
MUSICIANS
COCK (Alive or stuffed)

The play is in two acts.

La Justice

or

The Cock That Crew

Prolog to Act I

[Spoken by the JUDGE*]*

Half light in theater. The JUDGE *steps out before the curtain or on stage in street clothes. Spot. As he recites, he dresses himself in his court robes, wig, etc.*

>Dear friends and followers of the stage,
>I greet you in a barbarous age.
>I wish you peace and brief repose
>As you pursue where drama goes.
>My intentions, as you might guess,
>Are high; I shall not give you less
>Than you deserve, despite my pay,
>Asking only to have my say.
>We seek, of course, some point of truth,
>But if the truth be known, forsooth,
>It is that eye deceives and words
>Are but the flights of fickle birds.
>What, then? Where do we turn to know
>God's grace in our geometry?
>Where the naked heart in our theology?
>
>Foremost I must ask indulgence
>For a meagre tongue; refulgence
>Is the gift of living in fog
>And patiently keeping a log.
>We often falsely clear the mist,
>Ignorant of the truth we've missed.

[House lights slowly down]

> This theater's lights, in turning dark,
> Help us, willingly, lose our mark,
> That we in darkness may unite
> Our hearts and, losing our minds, ignite.
> Yield me, then, your mind's perspective;
> Cease, tonight, to be protective
> Of your money, honor, and life,
> And even, if the need arises, your wife.
> We aim to please, to have our fun,
> Even though, when the night is done,
> You may feel your virtue's ravished
> With no pleasure being lavished.
>
> So be it, a writer's task is hard,
> His work perhaps a tub of lard
> Within which he beats in vain
> And causes everyone a pain.
> For which reason, do not seek me out;
> I have pressing engagements, or gout.
> And, in passing, let me thank
> Good fellows Rockefeller and Guggenheim,
> Who though they cannot make a rhyme
> Do pay me *something* for my time.
> There, now. I'm dressed. I've had my say;
> So let's get on with this damned play.

[Lights out. Music]

ACT ONE

The set is a courtroom, out of which, at certain points, the JUDGE'S *bedroom and dining room also. The jury box, within which the* JURY, *some of whom are* MUSICIANS, *is sealed and, preferably, near the* AUDIENCE, *who are the courtroom spectators. The angles of the set, as of the play, are asymmetric, the ambience claustrophobic. Stage lights up. An* ATTENDANT *enters from the rear, pounds the floor three times with a staff.*

ATTENDANT: Oyez, oyez, oyez! the court will please rise!

> *[He can repeat this. The* AUDIENCE *rises or not. Processional music. From behind the* AUDIENCE *the people of the play enter, in reverse order of importance. One of them carries a cage with a* COCK *in it. Their court attire is a miscellany, from the drab to the courtly, from the rumpled suits of forgotten fashion to the splendor of wigs and gowns. There is something of both the royal court and the church processional here, the higher functionaries perhaps smiling and nodding benignly to some of the* AUDIENCE *as they pass. They all take their positions on stage and remain standing. The* JUDGE *enters from elsewhere, the music stops. The* ATTENDANT *pounds the floor three times.]*

This court is now in session, the Honorable Judge *[Indistinguishable]* presiding, *[Rapidly]* Section Three of the Fourth Division of the Lower Appellate, Eastern Diocese, Fourth Term, Hanoverian, Co-Terminal in the three hundred and sixty-forth Assize, Department Seven, the *State*—

JUDGE: *[Gaveling once]* Good. Good. Excellently done. And a clear, clear day at last.

ATTENDANTS: *[Mumbling]* Hear, hear. . . .

> *[the* JUDGE *sits. Everyone on stage sits. The* AUDIENCE, *if standing, also]*

JUDGE: *[Waving his hand desultorily]* Let the jury enter.

ATTENDANT: *[Continuing pompously]* —Department Seven, the *STATE* versus—

JUDGE: *[Gaveling once, irritated]* Let the jury enter.

> *The jury box bursts open, and the* JURY's *heads and torsos spill over and out. They are closely bunched, rather like a cluster of over-bright flowers, leaning, twisting, and turning at odd angles within their window. They are in white-face, with bright red lips and cheeks, have elaborate hair styles, and wear ballroom finery at least a century out of date. Throughout the play they jerk and*

bobble and gabble like a collection of e.g. balloon-heads, geese,
puppets, spastics, irrepressible children. They have fans, hand-
kerchiefs, decanters and goblets, etc. During the play they take
snuff, spray perfume, smoke from long-stemmed holders, clean
lorgnettes, leer, stare, and make faces at the cast and AUDIENCE,
read newspapers, drink wine and eat delicacies, occasionally
burp and pass air, titter, yawn, doze, try out make-up, disguises,
masks, etc. They are given to interruption, shows of approbation
and disapproval, e.g. tapping fans on sill, and digression; also
mockery, pun, outrageous "wit." Their lines often overlap the
regular dialog, just as the JUDGE'*s gaveling overlaps theirs. They*
may tune their instruments occasionally or punctuate with them.
Now and then, one or more of them come out of the box to dance
or get water, e.g. from a cooler, or to display himself perhaps.
Their particular lines, which are simply noted in the text, are
assigned by the director, who while encouraging a certain anar-
chic and libidinous spontaneity in them must also control and,
above all, orchestrate them. One of them is a "silly"; another is a
"dummy," given to inchoate sounds of mirth, anger, rebuttal, etc.,
throughout the play. Otherwise, a spread of age, fat and thin,
male and female, voice, etc. At least ten, but as many as twenty.
A chandelier in the box, and lush red walls, on one of which a
mirror.

JURY: Why, look at that cock!
        The size of it!
        Where? I can't see any cock.
        My dear, you never see cock.
            [They laugh]
        At all, at all. Do you have a bobby pin dear?
        He *must* be guilty.
        Who?
        Have you no imagination?
        Of course! It's written all over his face!
            [They laugh]

JUDGE: *[Gaveling patiently]* Order. Order.

JURY: But of course, darling! We must have order. It's *essential.* Order
is the visible paradigm of civilization. I feel it in every arthritic bone.

[Shushing the others, e.g. tapping their noses with fan] Tut! Tut! Come on, now, you silly ganders. Tut, tut! *[They shush each other. Silence]*

JUDGE: *[Smiling]* The bench is pleased. The bench agrees with you. Order is indeed necessary. The bench finds your perception exemplary.

ATTENDANTS: *[Mumbling]* Hear, hear. . . .

> *[The JURY titters excitedly from the flattery. The JUDGE raises his hand to silence them]*

JUDGE: *[Smiling and nodding to the PROSECUTOR]* Are you ready, sir? You may, if so, proceed with the charge. I sense, sir, it will be a good day.

ATTENDANTS: *[Mumbling]* Hear, hear. . . .

JURY: What? *No introduction? [He is abruptly shushed]* But I don't even know— *[He is shushed again. The PROSECUTOR clears his throat, then several of the JURY, then the JUDGE, as warning. More shushes]*

PROSECUTOR: *[Standing by the cock]* If it please the court—

JURY: *[Bursting out laughing]*
Oh, bravo, bravo!
Simply marvelous!
So well educated!
And *do* look at his cock!
Oh, at last a cock I can see.

> *[They laugh again. The JUDGE gavels]*

PROSECUTOR: If it please the court— *[He pauses, expecting another outburst. There is none]* —the person before you *[Everyone looks, but no one appears designated as the defendant]* is accused, I say *accused*—

JURY: Oh, good point. *Probing.*
Intense.
I do hope he's going to say *de facto* soon.

PROSECUTOR: —of a crime than which there is none more vile to man. To man, I say.

JURY: *[Gasps]*
        Oh, dear, dear!
        What *does* he mean?
        Guilty by all means!
        What person is he talking about?

[The JUDGE *gavels]*

PROSECUTOR: We intend to demonstrate—

JURY: *With* the cock, I hope. Is his name Robin? *[Titters]* Off with his cock!
[They laugh, then shush each other]

PROSECUTOR: —beyond any reasonable doubt that during the night in question the accused was A. *active,* B. *on the premises,* and *ipso facto* in consequence, C. *the guilty party*!

[Brief music]

JURY: *Ta-da!*
        Did someone say *party*?
        A *guilty* party. *Ipso facto*, indeed.
        What? Guilty? Already? *[Rapping the sill and giggling]* Even better. I *adore* guilty parties. Some of my best experiences have been born, so to speak, at guilty parties.
        [They laugh]

JUDGE: *[Gaveling. To* PROSECUTOR*]* The Prosecutor will confine his remarks to . . . to a brief outline at this time. The bench is . . . indulgent, but to a point only. To a particular point only. We wish to conclude the case . . . before nightfall—before, that is, darkness descends upon us.

ATTENDANTS: *[Mumbling]* Hear, hear . . . .

[Brief ominous music]

JURY: Oh, hear, *hear*.
        What a fine, fine man.
        What *time* is the guilty party?

DEFENSE: *[Rising]* Objection, your honor!

JURY: *You* object? *Who*, pray tell, are *you*? Your clothes are a positive illumination of your low, *low* connections, I'm sure.

DEFENSE: The question is irrelevant. Time is *immaterial*. I am the *Defense*, Your Honor. I stand on my perquisites and—

JUDGE: Ahh! Indeed, indeed. I agree *in toto*. Of course. *But*—the sun, I am afraid, moves apace.

ATTENDANTS: *[Mumbling]* Hear, hear . . . .

PROSECUTOR: *We* object! *We* exercise our right to object!

> *[Excited buzzing in the court. The* JUDGE *confers with his* AT-TENDANTS*]*

JURY: A crux already.
I think that cock is very nervous. Or paralyzed.
But I distinctly saw him twitch.
Not good enough.
What do you think of the cock's comb? *[Laughs outrageously]*
Rub it, my dear, and you'll soon find out.

> *[The* JUDGE *gavels]*

JUDGE: The objection is sustained! In the interests of progress, the objection is sustained. *[Both sides are congratulated by their aides, as is always the case]* The Prosecution and Defense will confine themselves to points of order, points of law, points of information, and in general . . . only . . . *relevant points.*

> *[Excitement and satisfaction everywhere]*

ATTENDANTS: Hear, hear . . . .

JURY: Hear, hear!
Point of order!
Information, please. —Oh, how I do love it!
Exciting. Exciting.
[They laugh]

JUDGE: *[Gaveling]* You may proceed, Prosecutor. As you can hear, excitement is *in the air.* The bench is pleased with our progress. The bench—

ATTENDANTS: *[Mumbling]* Hear, hear . . . .

PROSECUTOR: During the night in question, the accused, a being wholly devoid of morality and sentience—

JURY: *Sentience?* What is that?

PROSECUTOR: —of his own volition—

JURY: *His?*
       Volition?
       Shhh!

PROSECUTOR: —did perpetrate the aforesaid crime!

JURY: *[Gleefully clapping]* Oh, guilty, guilty!
       Hang the dog and be done!
       I *love* aforesaid.
       And *I* love aforeskin.
       Off with his cock!
       Capital, capital!
       [They laugh. The JUDGE *gavels]*

JUDGE: The bench would like to repair an oversight. The bench has domestic troubles. The bench must soon go home for lunch. The bench does not know what lunch is. The bench . . . has never known what lunch is.

[Pause]

JURY: Why, the poor man.
       Such unvarnished honesty.
       I, for one, am giving him my full attention.

JUDGE: *[Abruptly]* So be it. For the prosecution—Oswaldo Kroner, D.B.S.S. and *Diplomate de Corpus,* University Kantzbergen. *[Music. The* PROSECUTOR *bows. His* ASSISTANTS *clap politely]* For the Defense—Mon-

sieur Gary de Flange, Ps. B. de S. and *Croqueur Extraordinaire* de Nance.
[Music. The DEFENSE *rises and bows. Polite applause from his* ASSISTANTS*]*

JURY: I do hope at least one of them can sing.
If he can't sing you can be sure he's circumcised..
[They laugh]

JUDGE: *[Gaveling]* And now, dear, dear friends, we proceed! *Justice proceeds apace. [Music. Applause]* Thank you, thank you. The bench is recovered. The bench feels . . . *vital.* Yes . . . *vital.*

ATTENDANTS: *[Mumbling]* Hear, hear . . . .

> *[More applause. Court* ATTENDANTS *shake his hand. The* JUDGE *holds out his arm to the* JURY. A slightly confused chord]

JURY: *[Referring to the chord]* Well. More or less.
Whatever.
Have we progressed very far yet?

PROSECUTOR: *[Pompously]* Crime, ladies and gentlemen? *Crime does not pay.* —Or does it? You will ask the question? But who will answer it? There on his high seat rests a judge. Will *he* answer your question? *[The* JUDGE *chuckles and nods]*

JURY: Bogged down in domestic morass.

PROSECUTOR: Somewhere in this courtroom is the accused. Will *he* answer your question?

JURY: Assuredly not.
I, for one, would never ask any such question.

PROSECUTOR: Across directly *[He points]* , learned counsel for the defense. Will *he* answer your question?

> *[Pause]*

JURY: Answer, you dummy.
I think he's terribly presumptuous.

I think he's cute.
But so savage.
[They giggle. The JUDGE *gavels]*

PROSECUTOR: *Will God himself answer your question?*

JURY: Good heavens. A quantum leap.

PROSECUTOR: We have before us, you and I, a very human situation.

JURY: Excellent.
Yes, do let us be *humane* about it.

PROSECUTOR: On the one hand, the wife, the children. The grandmother. The dog, the cat. Pain, sickness, heartache, struggle, death.

JURY: No more?
Yes, how about dirty underwear?

PROSECUTOR: On the other hand—yes, *on the other hand,* what do we have? *What do we have?*

JURY: Do tell.

PROSECUTOR: We have the man. We have the stranger. We have the strange utterings of an unknown tongue. You have the night. *[Pause]* We have the vain reachings of hands, like the flight of two thousand crows in the dark. *[He demonstrates]*

JURY: Now *that* definitely rings a bell, I think. Two thousand Baltimore orioles and my mind would be an absolute blank.

PROSECUTOR: The tangled passions of we mortals feeble!

JURY: Oh, how I love a tangled passion.

PROSECUTOR: I repeat—*we mortals feeble.*

JURY: It wasn't that good to begin with.

PROSECUTOR: The Prosecution will prove beyond any reasonable expectation—

JURY: I really question the *any.*
        And the *reasonable.*
        I won't have *any* expectation.

DEFENSE: I object. *We* object. It is a leading question, a leading statement,
a leading situation.
                    [The JURY *laughs through this. The* JUDGE *gavels]*

JURY: It's compromising also, don't you think? *[They laugh]*

DEFENSE: We demand a ruling from the bench. The Prosecution has over-
reached—

JURY: Overstepped.
        Exceeded.
        And transgressed.
        Stepped in a pile of shit.

PROSECUTOR: *[Loudly, silencing everyone]* Your honor, I rest on my laurels!

        [Everyone is motionless. The PROSECUTOR *suddenly begins a fast
        tap step, quickly stopped by the* JUDGE's *gaveling and the* JURY*]*

JURY: Uh-uh-uh!
        Stop that, you pig!
        No passion!
        We are here to dissect, not drool.
        How well you've said it. —But don't say it again.

        [The PROSECUTOR *stares briefly, then walks stiffly to his table,
        where his* ASSISTANTS *pat his back, put a sweater over his
        shoulders, touch up his hair, etc. much like a fighter between
        rounds or an actor between acts]*

JUDGE: Is the Defense ready? The bench is most anxious. Time—*[He looks
about himself a bit desperately]*

ATTENDANTS: *[Mumbling]* Hear, hear . . . .

        [The DEFENSE *and his* ASSISTANTS *file out]*

DEFENSE: We are, Your Grace. We *are* ready.

[The JUDGE *is flattered]*

JURY: *[Cackling] Your Eminence!*
Your Worthiness!
Your Abstraction!
And Your Indefinabilitiness!
Old cabbage soup, he used to be called, when he played rugby.
Gorgeous.
[The JUDGE *gavels]*

JUDGE: The bench accepts the compliments. The bench is deserving. —
But oh, how the bench *suffers!*— Proceed, Defense Attorney. *[As the*
DEFENSE *speaks, his* ASSISTANTS *form many-headed, many-limbed, con-
torted tableaus, using whatever props they need]*

DEFENSE: The Defense will build, erect, and solidify upon *guilt and
innocence.*

JURY: Very proper.

DEFENSE: Hearsay will not be a factor.

JURY: Again, very proper. I like this man.

*[*DEFENSE *clears his throat]*

DEFENSE: In all situations in life there is—

JURY: A negligible factor.

DEFENSE: —the accused—

JURY: Bravo.

DEFENSE: —and the accuser, the tormented—

JURY: *Very deep.*

DEFENSE: —and his tormentor—

JURY: Sainted sassefras!

DEFENSE: *[Pointing]* —the up and the down.

> *[The first tableau, illustrating his words. A* DEFENSE
> ASSISTANT *rushes forward and recites bombastically]*

ASSISTANT: Behold, my friends, this topsy-turvy,
One head pox, the other scurvy;
The others who can say what ails;
Perhaps they've eaten cans of snails.
> *[He laughs and returns to his table]*

JURY: It's going metaphysical much too quickly.
It was all right until the up and down. He definitely lost me
there.
Does it move?
No, no, it's utterly frozen.
But it does provoke idle thoughts.

> *[The tableau breaks and begins to form another, as the*
> DEFENSE *continues]*

DEFENSE: I have not come here to save the accused. Nor have I come here
to save *you.*
> *[The* JURY *look at one another, pop-eyed and pointing to*
> *themselves and the* AUDIENCE*]*

I have come to save *myself.*

JURY: *Indeed.*
A complete stroke. How wondrous.
And we do hope you've informed your client.

DEFENSE: In saving myself, I shall save *not* the accused, ladies and
gentlemen, *not* the bench, the Prosecution, the court itself—I shall save
the world. —*Salvation [He points to tableau #2]* is the name of my game.

DEFENSE ASSISTANT: Ah, here's a soothing wondrous sight
To guide us through the darkest night;
Bleed freely, smile or smirk;
But never fail to do God's work.

JURY: Work? I thought I heard *game.*

Game? Does it go with *party?*
I'm game for *any* game.
Oh, putt-putt. Shove it or stow it.
I adore that fourth head.
From the left or the right?
With the *grimace.*
And does this one move?
It collapses, I think. Like a bleeding black hole.
Tsk.

*[The tableau collapses, begins quickly to form its final con-
figuration]*

DEFENSE: And so, I ask you—do you bleed? do you wonder? do you fear death that comes on dainty poodle legs?

JURY: He's really getting me in my gut.

[Tableau #3 is "Death on Dainty Poodle Legs"]

DEFENSE ASSISTANT: Look! Oh, look! Turn not your head
From this vision of you dead;
We mortals must the mirror seek
That through the veil will let us peek.

JURY: What utter horse shit.

DEFENSE: *[Perorating]* Thus I shall contend. To my last breath I shall contend. It is foregone and written that I shall weaken. *[He lies on the final tableau]* My body shall rot! I shall rage, rage, ladies and gentlemen, at the putrescence of my expiration. But also shall I sing at my long demise, leave you, so to speak, with song, as should we all, as should we all.

[The tableau moves slowly away]

JURY: Oh. This one moves.
Tableau vivant.
Orgosolo furioso!
Bean curd and tomatoes!

DEFENSE: Hear me! *[He sings something indefinable, operatic]* Hear my song! *[He sings]*

JURY: Oh, my gut.

DEFENSE: Hear the sweetness of it, the beauty, the strength! *[He sings]*

JURY: Defense singing while being borne off on the wings of Death on Dainty Poodle Legs. *[They join the* PROSECUTOR *in mangled song. The* JUDGE *gavels. With each gavel, the lights dim progressively. The tableau fades]*

JUDGE: Sold! I declare this particular action sold! It is sold. For cash, barter, or services rendered, this tableau is sold! It is sold! I tell you, sold without recall. *[Nearly dark]* And I declare this court in recess for the bench to take his lunch *en famille! The sun still shines!*

ATTENDANTS: *[Mumbling]* Hear, hear . . . .

JUDGE: —Nadia! Nadia!

> *[Blackout. Music. Lights up on the* JUDGE'*s dining room, where the* JUDGE, *his* WIFE, SON, *and* DAUGHTER *are eating. They speak with a vague mid-European accent]*

DAUGHTER: Papa. Are you really our father?

WIFE: Ilke! Eat your soup. *[To her husband]* Did you hear? Children have no respect today.

JUDGE: Of course, my dear. But what did she mean?

WIFE: Mean? Who knows what she means? —Listen, husband. We need new crockery. It is essential for our well being, our . . . *self-esteem.*

JUDGE: Didn't we just buy new crockery?

WIFE: Bah. It is all *cracked.* The *crockery* is *cracked.* The children are careless. Everybody is careless with the crockery.

JUDGE: *[Screaming at the* CHILDREN*] Why are you so careless?* Do you know what prices are? I am a civil servant. My salary is fixed! *[Pause] I* am fixed! Do you hear! I cannot *move!*

DAUGHTER: A true father would not scream at us like that. Who are these men you send here every day?

JUDGE: *[Nervously to his* WIFE*]* What men? What men is she talking about that I send here every day?

WIFE: Bah. Forget the men, husband. What about the crockery?

JUDGE: *[Shouting]* We cannot afford the crockery! We will eat from the cracked crockery!

WIFE: *[Scornfully]* It will not be very *esthetic*. And what if we have *guests*?

JUDGE: *Guests*? what are *guests*? What *guests* should we have?

SON: The window cleaner, Papa.

JUDGE: What? The window cleaner?

DAUGHTER: *[Lewdly]* The milk man, Papa.

JUDGE: *Milk man? [To* WIFE*]* What do they mean? Are they crazy? Who are these people?

WIFE: The milk man must be paid, no?

JUDGE: What? What are you talking about? Of course the milk man must be paid. *[Snarling at the* CHILDREN*]* *Why do you drink so much milk?* I cannot stand this consumption of milk! Milk is bad for you!

SON: Papa, we must grow.

JUDGE: You grow too big! Everything grows too big! I am surrounded by pigs! *[He pauses, collects himself]*

WIFE: Come, come, husband. Eat your soup. How does your trial go?

JUDGE: *[Scoffing]* Bah. Trial. I cannot tell the Prosecutor from the Defense. We have a cock that will not talk. And my jury conspires.

WIFE: Ahh, conspires? Against whom, may I ask you?

JUDGE: Hah. That is the question, is it not? *Who conspires against whom?*

Oh, if we only knew. If only *I* knew. Some of them are *swine*. I am sure of it.

DAUGHTER: Papa. What is this cock you speak of?

[The SON *crows briefly]*

WIFE: It is not a good situation, then?

JUDGE: Hah. *[Laughing, good-naturedly]* Who knows what a good situation is, eh . . . Coo-coo? *[He chucks her under the chin playfully and laughs]* Eh?

DAUGHTER: Papa. There is a boy at the school who wants to study with me.

JUDGE: *[To* WIFE*]* Listen. We have time. Come into the bedroom with me.

WIFE: But the bed is made.

SON: Papa. Give me money for candy.

JUDGE: *[Grabbing his wife's leg]* We can do it on the floor. Forget the bed!

WIFE: Husband, the children are watching.

DAUGHTER: I don't think this boy wants really to study.

JUDGE: *[Moving his hand up her leg]* We can shut the door. We can shut the door, yes?

SON: Papa. The dentist says my teeth are rotten.

WIFE: You will wrinkle your suit.

JUDGE: It is already wrinkled!

WIFE: *[Pushing him away]* Wrinkled? It is already *wrinkled*? How can that be? I just this morning ironed out all the wrinkles. How did you get wrinkles in your suit?

JUDGE: *Forget the wrinkles!*

WIFE: But I ironed it. This morning I ironed it. Don't you understand?

JUDGE: What? You ironed my wrinkles? —But how can that be? Didn't
I—

WIFE: *Precisely*, husband. *How can that be? [Angrily]* I work my fingers
to the bone to keep your suit without wrinkles. Day and night I iron.

JUDGE: But I never see you iron.

WIFE: What does that matter? Do you doubt my word? Are you calling me
a liar, husband?

DAUGHTER: Papa. I do not trust this boy. He is always licking his lips and
moving his fingers. But he is very persistent. My friend Helga says that
he wants something from inside my pants. Papa. What do you think he
wants?

SON: Papa. I got one hundred percent in spelling today. I can spell
corkscrew.

> *[The* COURT *begins to stir. Lights coming up slowly on it]*

JURY: So he thinks we *conspire.* Dear, dear.
All swine conspire.
Dear, dear again.

> *[A loud buzzer]*

JUDGE: *[Rising]* I must go. A quick dance, then.

JURY: Lovely.
I could use a diversion.

> *[The* JUDGE *puts a tango on the record machine and dances]*

JUDGE: Come, Nadia.

JURY: Yes, do come, Nadia.

JUDGE: Dance with me, Nadia. Just one minute. *[He grabs her desperately. She dances reluctantly]* Ah, do you remember when we were young?

WIFE: *[Softening]* Do you think I am so old, then? Huh?

JUDGE: *[Grabbing her buttocks]* Not yet. Not yet, Nadia. There is still time. There is still time.

JURY: While there's meat, there's time.
Oh, dear, yes. Old Nadia's still good for a bite or two.
[They laugh]

JUDGE: *[Urgently]* Nadia. My suit is already wrinkled. Come with me into the bedroom. We will have an *Anschluss,* yes? a *blitzkrieg?* a one-two-three boom-boom?

WIFE: No.

JUDGE: Yes?

WIFE: No.

SON: *[To his* SISTER*]* Look at Papa dance.

DAUGHTER: I am already looking at Papa dance.

SON: Look how he holds our mother.

JURY: Yes, do look.
Do look at the old cock dance.
How drab.
I've heard she knocks off a bit on the side.
Darling, the milk must be paid, you know.
[They laugh]

JUDGE: *Nadia.*

WIFE: No! Tonight. Tonight I will go with you to the bedroom.

JUDGE: *[Laughing]* You promise?

WIFE: I give you my word.

JUDGE: In the bed? We will do it in the bed?

WIFE: Wherever you like. In the closet even.

JUDGE: *[With glee]* You mean it? In the closet? With the shoes even, maybe? On the floor?

WIFE: *[Tired of him]* Yes. Yes. Ski boots. Umbrellas. Anything. Get back to work. Get back to your trial. You have *responsibility.*

JURY: Oh, yes, yes.
Oh, do, do.
And shut off that music.
[A loud buzzer]

ATTENDANT: *[Pounding staff]* The court is now resumed.

SON: Papa. Papa, what is the glory that was Greece?

DAUGHTER: Papa. What shall I tell him?

JUDGE: Nadia—give me a parting message.

WIFE: *Think about the crockery*

JUDGE: *[Joyfully]* I shall. I shall. I promise you I shall think about the crockery. Ah, what sweet mystery in those words. *[He hastily puts on his wig and robes, takes his seat, gazes at the* AUDIENCE*]* Next witness, please.

JURY: We haven't even heard the first, my dear.
Don't we get any charge to the jury?
A few words?
A smile?
Hmph.

JUDGE: Very well, very well. The bench is inclined, at this point, to . . . *frivolity.* The bench is *excited.* — Is it that spring is in the air? A touch of . . .?

ATTENDANTS: *[Mumbling]* Hear, hear. . . .

> *[The following speech by the* JUDGE *builds to a passionate exhortation. The* "DUMMY," *particularly, reacts to it]*

JUDGE: My ladies and gentlemen of the jury, you have heard the opening statements. You will now take note of the evidence presented. Above all things, keep an open mind. And remember always, *a fortiori, speculum causa,* and, *horrible visu,* the party of two parts.

JURY: When *is* that tiresome party going to be?

JUDGE: Weigh on the one hand and on the other. Consult not your prejudices. Act herein with the innocence of angels, cutting off heads and shaking hands with equal tranquility. Yours is the sweet role of the Divine Executor Himself. Have dignity but no pride. Fatten not your egos on dreams of power. Fill not your bellies on foul lust—

JURY: It *sounds* like a party, but I'm sure it isn't.

JUDGE: List not to the whisperings of the vulgar throng. I empower you with grace, wisdom, patience, and divinity. Judge, and I swear ye shall not in turn be judged. For mine is the power and yours shall be the glory ever more, here and in all—

JURY: Stop! My god, stop! I'll never bear it!
I'm gagged and agog! Good heavens.
How we *do* earn our keep.
[Pause]
Well. I certainly am flattered.
It doesn't take much to flatter a jackass, dear.
Nasty!
Brute!
[They fight briefly, until the others break it up]
Oh, do let's get back to our nobility.
Is there any more, Judge?

JUDGE: Yes—Remember the crockery. *[He laughs abruptly]* —Oh, how I suffer!

ATTENDANTS: *[Mumbling]* Hear, hear . . . .

JURY: He's crazy.
Buggers.
Absolutely.

JUDGE: *[Gaveling] First witness. First witness.*

JURY: Oh, good line. That's two so far.

> *[Lively music. A middle-aged "stock" Jew does a quick vaude-ville entrance. He is elemental, baffling, ultimately frightening, striking out from beneath the stereotype]*

JEW: Sooo? Who's gonna give me the third degree, huh?

JURY: How disagreeable.
It's a court of *law*, stupid, not a police station.
[They laugh]

JEW: Hey, you got a face just like an egg. You want a pill?

> *[The JURY laughs]*

JUDGE: Identify yourself, please.

JURY: Egg. *[They laugh. The JUDGE gavels]*

JEW: Why not? You got an honest face, even if you don't look like an egg. *[He and the JURY laugh]* —But I still wouldn't trust you with the baby. *[Again, he and the JURY laugh, as if at a very funny joke]*

JURY: *[Happily]*
We're with you, Jew. We're with you.
At last a little life.

JEW: —That's right. You hit the hammer right on the head. I'm the Jew. You get it? A money lender—you feel a song coming on? —Like a good bowel movement, huh? *[He laughs]* A chicken flucker. Cut me, I bleed. *[He laughs]* You get it—cut me, I bleed.

JURY: Oh, we get it, Jew.
Hilarious.
A born comic.
Cut me, I bleed.
Somebody cut his throat quick.
[They laugh]

JUDGE: *[Gaveling]* The witness will confine himself to facts. The witness will realize it is already past lunch. —*And our luck holds. Our luck holds.*

ATTENDANTS: *[Mumbling]* Hear, hear . . . .

JEW: *[Humoring the* JUDGE*]* Sure. Okay, the facts. The facts are gonna speak for themselves, right? The facts are always gonna speak for themselves. That is the ABC of every legal system in the whole wide world.

DEFENSE: Objection!

JURY: That man is getting on my nerves.

JEW: Oiii, I got an objection already. Maybe *I* got a couple objections, too, huh?

JURY: If it comes to that, *we* have objections also.
For example, I—

JUDGE: *[Gaveling]* Overruled. All objections overruled.

JEW: And what about *sustentions?* You gonna leave 'em out?

JUDGE: Mr. Prosecutor, have you any questions for this witness?

JEW: *Right.* All I need is opportunity.

PROSECUTOR: *[Stepping forth condescendingly]* Now, Jew *[The* JURY *squeals in delight]*, on the night in question—

JEW: You're not gonna ask me if I'm married? —Say, you got a license, even? —A clean shirt? —What university did you populate?

PROSECUTOR: —on the night in question—

JEW: Oi, what a night that was. You should a been there. There was fat Rosie with the Rabbi in a pickle, big as life. You getting the picture?

JURY: We're getting it, Jew.
Fat Rosie and the Rabbi in a big pickle.

JEW: Oi, what a perception you got. With a jury like that, who needs an electric chair?

[They laugh. The JUDGE *gavels]*

PROSECUTOR: *[Pointing, as he single-mindedly continues]* Jew, where were you, what were you doing, and whom with?

JEW: Whom with? *Whom with.* Hey, what kind of guy you think I am? You think I would do anything *whom with? [Jabbing with his finger]* Whom with! Whom with! —That's what your professors taught you? You're gonna give me a complex. Bowels, even.

JURY: Oh, tell him, Jew, tell him.
We're with you.
Oi, yes, indeed.

PROSECUTOR: I repeat, Jew, where were you, what were—

JEW: You don't think that's a leading question? —And where's it gonna lead? I'll tell you where it's gonna lead. You're gonna ruin the reputation of a wonderful woman and mother, that's where it's gonna lead.

JURY: Oh, *dear.*
That's bad.
But *interesting.*
La femme at last. At the bottom of every case you find one.
I am absolutely *intent. [Leans forward and looks through lorgnette]*

PROSECUTOR: Her name?

JEW: *[To* JUDGE*]* Your Honor, I gotta divulge this? Such an exterminatin' fact?

JURY: *[Mimicking]*
Yer Honor, I gotta divulge this?
Such an exterminatin' fact?

JEW: Listen, I got a mountain yodel you would never believe. You never heard of a Jewish goat herder? They got 'em all over Switzerland. *[To* PROSECUTOR*]* Don't worry, I'm gonna stick to the facts.

[He yodels. The JURY *yodels. They yodel back and forth. The* PROSECUTOR *places the caged* COCK *in front of the witness. The yodeling stops abruptly]*

JURY: Oh dear. That cock again.
          So naked.
          And red.
          Dis-gusting.

JUDGE: Mr. Prosecutor, is this . . . *relevant*. The bench confesses a certain . . . *curiosity*. Where . . . is this leading us? —And how soon? *How soon? [He looks around axiously]*

ATTENDANTS: *[Mumbling]* Hear, hear . . . .

PROSECUTOR: Your Honor, the cock is essential.

JURY: How true.
          A frank statement.

JEW: Hmmm, so maybe you got a point?

JURY: Oh, true, Jew, true. Verily and true.

PROSECUTOR: The Prosecution intends to prove the defendant guilty. On the night in question, this cock—

JEW: Two minutes. I could fluck it in two minutes. I was in a contest once. I'm a champion flucker.

JURY: Oh, we're with you, Jew. Fluck away with thine nimble fingers.

PROSECUTION: —was in the alley known as Shinbone Alley.

JURY: *[Singing]* Oh, de shinbone connected to de—
          [The JUDGE *gavels]*
          Philistine. Anyone for bridge?
          Proceed, Jew. Remember. We're with you.

JEW: Proceed? Me? You're asking me, a member of the Socialist Worker's Party, to proceed? Listen, all I got is a dance, maybe. I got a soul full of dance.

PROSECUTOR: *[Insistently] Do you recognize this cock?*

JURY: Can't *stand* that word.

JEW: Get him to talk maybe. His voice I might recognize. *[The* PROSECUTOR *shakes the cage]* More. I can't hear a thing. *[The* PROSECUTOR pokes the COCK*]* Maybe he's dead? I never forget a cock's crow.

JURY: A cock's crow. Did you hear—a cock's crow.

JUDGE: *[To the* PROSECUTOR*]* Can the Prosecutor simulate? —I'm afraid the dawn is long since passed.

ATTENDANTS: *[Mumbling]* Hear, hear . . . .

JURY: Oh, simulate indeed.

> *[The* PROSECUTOR *clears his throat]*

PROSECUTOR: *[Simulating]* Puk. Puk, puk, puk, puk! Puk, puk, puk!

JEW: Do it like you was wringing his neck.

JURY: Yes, do something. You sound positively castrated.

PROSECUTOR: *[As directed]* Puk, puk! PUK! PUK! PUK!

JEW: *[Throttling the* PROSECUTOR*]* Oomph. Give it more oomph.

JURY: Fluck him, Jew, fluck him.

PROSECUTOR: *[Frantically]* PUK! PUK! PUK! PUK! PUK! . . .

> *[The* JURY *sounds out a barnyard cacophony. The* JUDGE *gavels everyone silent]*

JUDGE: Well, do you recognize the cock, Jew? The cock that just crew? — My word!

JEW: *[With a brogue]* I never saw the bugger in me life.

JUDGE: Bugger?

JURY: Quaint. Quaint.
The cock that was a bugger.
The cock that was a bugger crew. *[He tries to sing the line as a ditty]*

> *[The* PROSECUTOR *tries to talk, cannot. An* ASSISTANT *steps forward]*

ASSISTANT: Your Honor, the Prosecution requests a brief recess.

DEFENSE: Objection!

JUDGE: Overruled. Sustained. I'll think about it. Gad! What time is it?

ATTENDANTS: *[Mumbling]* Hear, hear . . . .

JEW: Listen, I got a great dance number. *[Stepping down]* It's a good filler. That's what the world needs, good fillers.

JURY: Good cocks and good fillers, Jew!

JEW: C'mon, give me a beat, ladies. I can dance like a prince. *[Music. He begins to move rhythmically and sing]*

> I got the Pinsk blues.
> I got the Minsk green.
> I got a cock-a-doodle-doo
> Like you never seen.
> Oi-yoi-yoi-yoi-yoiiii!

JURY: Step it up, Jew!
Get some Russian into it!
Yes. Get some Russian in your coffee!
Why don't you show him, *dummkopf?*
Oh, I shall, I shall.

> *[He leaves the jury box and joins the* JEW. *Linking arms, they sing and dance. The music picks up]*

BOTH: We got the Pinsk blues.
We got the Minsk green.
We got a cock-a-doodle-doo

Like you never seen.
Oi-yoi-yoi-yoi-yoiiii!
[They pause]

JEW: Listen, Judge. You ever heard of a Jew milk man?

JUDGE: *Milk man? Milk?* That sounds so familiar. *[Clutching his chest]*
—Oh, how I suffer! Why? Why!— Nadia? —*Nadia?* . . . What is it about
milk—
[His WIFE enters, her arms full of shoes, etc.]
Nadia, have you ever heard of a Jew milk man? —What are you doing?

WIFE: I am cleaning out the closet.

JUDGE: *[Petulantly]* Damn you! I don't want the closet cleaned.

WIFE: *[Coldly]* And are *you* going to be on the bottom, husband, *yes?*

JUDGE: What? Bottom? What bottom? Why do you waste my *time?*

ATTENDANTS: *[Mumbling]* Hear, hear . . . .

WIFE: *And have you been thinking about the crockery?*

JEW: *Cracked.* I'm telling you it's *cracked.*

JUDGE: How do you know it's cracked, Jew? *How do you know about my
crockery?*

JEW: *[Shrugging]* So what's so personal?

JURY: Are you following this?

WIFE: *[Dropping her shoes and pointing to the cage]* Where did you get
that red cock, husband?

JUDGE: Why— Why— *You are making me suffer!*

ATTENDANTS: *[Mumbling]* Hear, hear . . . .

[The JEW and the JUROR link arms with the WIFE]

ALL THREE: We got the Pinsk blues.
                    We got the Minsk green.
                    We got a cock-a-doodle-doo
                    Like you never seen.
                    Oi-yoi-yoi-yoi-yoiiii!

JURY: Oh, screw the Pinsk blues. Let's get back to the cock.
        Oh, that word again.
        Delete the screw.

DEFENSE: Your Honor, the Defense wishes to question the witness.

        [The JUROR returns to the jury box, the JUDGE's WIFE picks up the shoes]

JUDGE: Nadia.

WIFE: What is it?

JUDGE: *[A bright idea]* Put the *children* in the closet.

WIFE: *And—?*

JUDGE: We'll use the *bed.*

WIFE: They'll hear, you fool. You know how you slobber over your sex. *[She leaves quickly]*

JUDGE: *[After her]* Kill them, then! *[He looks around distractedly]*

JURY: Bloodthirsty devil, isn't he?
        It's his training. Formal, I mean.
        All those torts, you know, forever *sucking* on *torts.*
        All judges be hanged.

JUDGE: *[Gaveling]* Is the witness ready?

        [The JEW puts on a donkey head]

JEW: Hee-haw! Hee-haw! —I got a Mexican number, too.

JURY: He isn't fooling *me* for a minute.

I thought he was going to be a *blackie.*
Symmetry be damned.

JEW:　Hee-haw!

JURY:　*[The* DUMMY, *excited]* Hee-haw! Hee-haw!

DEFENSE:　Your name, please.

JEW:　Hee-haw! Hee-haw!

JURY:　*[The* DUMMY*]* Hee-haw!
　　　　Ah, the facts of the case at last.
　　　　Thank god that cock is gone.
　　　　But never forgotten.

DEFENSE:　Your name, please.

JEW:　Hee-haw! Hee-haw!

JURY:　*[The* DUMMY*]* Hee-haw!
　　　　I do wish we had the yodeling back.
　　　　And *where* has the *party* gone?

DEFENSE:　*Your name, please.*

JEW:　Hee-haw! Hee-haw!

JURY:　*[The* DUMMY*]* Hee-haw! . . .
　　　　Oh, how splendid, Defense.
　　　　We *love* your affirmation.

JUDGE:　*[Gaveling] Hurry.* Please, *hurry.* My wife, my wife, my wife—
Nadia awaits.

JEW and　DUMMY:　Hee-haw! Hee-haw!

JUDGE:　*[Gaveling silence]* But— but—

JURY:　*[The* DUMMY*]* Hee-haw! . . .
　　　　Say it, say it!

DEFENSE: Your name, your name! —Hee-haw! Hee-haw!

JURY: You don't think he's out of character?
Aren't we all, darling?
Now *that's* provocative. It really is, you swine.

DEFENSE: *Your name, sir!*

JEW: Hee-haw! Hee-haw!

JURY: *[The* DUMMY*]* Hee-haw! . . .
Get him, Agamemnon.
Bite him dead.
Correct! Correct! What's in a name?
Give him the old Troy run-around.
I've never trusted a Greek. Certainly not with my virtue.
All Greeks suck.
[Wild laughter. The JUDGE *gavels]*

DEFENSE: Your name! Give us your name!

PROSECUTION: We object!

ALL: Hee-haw! Hee-haw!

JURY: Oh, dear, we're making progress!
I'm absolutely thrilled!
Look! Look! He's unmasking himself!
[The JEW *takes off the donkey head. A chord]*
Why, it's the Jew!
Shhh! He's going to speak.
Now *that* should thicken the soup.
Shhh.
[Silence]

JEW: Your Honor. Honesty compels me to confess I feel a song coming on.

JUDGE: But—

JURY: Splendid.

JEW: —But I'm going to suppress it in the interest of civilization.

[He passes air]

DEFENSE: *And* your profession?

JEW: Lately I been cleaning a lot of windows.

[Gasps]

JURY: *Windows.*
Oh, my god. How this plot thickens.
Can we bear it?
We must, we must.

JUDGE: *You clean windows, sir?*

JEW: *[Shrugging]* It's a living, no?

JUDGE: *It is not a living. It is not a living! —Nadia! Nadia! NADIA!*

JURY: *[The* DUMMY*]* Hee-haw! . . .
[Slapping him] Shhh!
Shhhh!

[The JUDGE's SON *and* DAUGHTER *run in]*

DAUGHTER: Papa. Mama is in the bedroom.

JUDGE: At this hour? Is dinner ready? When did she go in? How can it be time for dinner?

ATTENDANTS: Hear, hear . . . .

SON: Papa. I played soccer today.

DAUGHTER: Papa. Mama has been working in the closet. Look. Look at what she found.
[She holds up a basin]

JUDGE: What is it?

SON: Your wedding crockery, Papa!

JUDGE: *[Getting up]* What . . . pretty flowers it has.

DAUGHTER: But they're faded, Papa.

SON: Papa, when will we go to the country again? Will you get me a pony?

DAUGHTER: Papa. What shall I do with the crockery?

JUDGE: *[Descending]* Let me see it. Let me hold it.
[He takes it from her]

DAUGHTER: The flowers are faded, Papa.
[He hugs it gently]

JUDGE: It doesn't matter. *[Soft music]* They are beautiful flowers. *[He dances slowly]* Oh, Nadia. Nadia. What legs you had. What lips.

SON: Ilke, what does he mean?

DAUGHTER: Hush. *[Dancing with the* JUDGE *but not touching]* Tell me about her, Papa.

JUDGE: She was soft. We were young.

SON: Tell me, too, Papa.
[He joins the dance]

JUDGE: Every day, we had fresh flowers on the dinner table.

DAUGHTER: Was Mama very beautiful, Papa?

JUDGE: We were passionately in love, but tender, *tender.* Do you understand, my little virgin?

DAUGHTER: Papa. I'm getting older. I do understand. Will I die soon? I know what is in my pants.
[They laugh together]

SON: Papa. What is in her pants?

JUDGE: No, no, no. You're too young. But soon . . . .

SON: Do you promise me, Papa?

JUDGE: Yes, yes.

SON: And will you get me a pony?

> *[The* PROSECUTOR *rises abruptly]*

PROSECUTOR: *[Booming]* I object! I object to this folderol!

> *[The music and dancing stop. Momentary freeze]*

JURY: *[In the silence]*
Oh, *get him.*
Do, do.
Oh, da-de-do.

> *[The* DEFENSE *rushes to the* JEW *with the cage and sticks it aggressively in front of him]*

JEW: Boy, you sure got a lousy bedside manner. You got a badge, even?

JUDGE: Children! I'm coming home! —I'm in pain!

ATTENDANTS: *[Mumbling]* Hear, hear . . . .

JEW: Listen. I got an Albanian number I do, too. —Get that cock out of my face!

JUDGE: Children! I'm coming home with you!

JEW: You think I'm gonna argue?

JURY: Thank god.
Who else?
[Like hens] CUT-cut-cut-cut. CUT-cut-cut-cut . . . .
[The DUMMY*]* Hee-haw! . . .

> *[The* PROSECUTION *and* DEFENSE ASSISTANTS *join in. The* JUDGE, *dropping his robes, leaves with his children]*

ATTENDANT: Adjourned! Adjourned until nine o'clock tomorrow! This session is adjourned! The day is over!

ATTENDANTS: *[Mumbling]* Hear, hear . . . .

[The JEW *shrugs. Lights out]*

INTERMISSION

Prolog to Act II

[Spoken by the JUDGE*]*

> Act II always thickens the plot
> But doesn't tell you an awful lot.
> In five you might work it all out,
> Dispel confusion and resolve doubt—
> But why? To seat whom on what throne?
> Might we not be better with just a bone
> Than some monstrous false-gained creature
> Of whom we recognize every feature?
> The pussy purring in your lap
> Can close his jaws just like a trap,
> Whereas the bone on which I dote
> Will merely tickle in your throat—
> Unless, of course, it makes you choke.
> —Ahh, there's the rib, and there's my cloak.
> > *[He picks up his robes]*
> Don't wriggle overmuch, dear hearts;
> Although we actors act our parts,
> When every beastly scene is done,
> Why, just like you, we're all for fun.
> > *[Loud knocking]*
> So, on with the show; I hear a knocking,

And, please, don't ever think *I'm* mocking—
[Lights out, then up on Act II]

ACT II

The JUDGE's bedroom. His WIFE, in a sensual night gown, lies in bed waiting. She does not appear to hear the knocking. In this act, the pace accelerates, particularly as the scene shifts from courtroom to home and back. Further, the sense of merging is also increased. The JUDGE enters breathlessly, almost dancing, and gets into bed with her.

JUDGE: I know. I know. I'm late. Well, I've been busy, busy, busy, busy as the proverbial bee. But I've come at last for my honey, eh? Eh? *[Poking her and chuckling]* Back to the hive, eh? Ahh, how young your breasts still look. What a marvel.

WIFE: *[Angrily]* My mother had cancer of the breast at fifty-two.

JUDGE: A mere picadillo. —But I don't recall your mother's having cancer. Is she still alive?

WIFE: *[Stiffly]* Yes. They cut it off. She is in a home. With other women like herself. I visit her.

JUDGE: What the devil is all that noise?

WIFE: None of them have breasts.

JUDGE: How strange.

WIFE: Some of them are in *jars*. I have seen them. Big ones, little—

JUDGE: I can't hear a word you say. *What* is that racket?

WIFE: The children. They are in the closet.

JUDGE: But I thought *we* were supposed to be in the closet.

WIFE: There were too many things in the closet.

JUDGE: You didn't clean it out?

WIFE: Why are you questioning me thus?

JUDGE: *[Placatingly]* Nadia. —May I touch your left breast?

WIFE: No. The right. Touch the right one.

SON: Papa! Let us out!

JUDGE: *[Fondling his* WIFE*]* Be still, my son. Be patient.

SON: Papa! There is no air!

JUDGE: *[Angrily]* Be still!
            [The knocking and pounding stop]
        Nadia. Do you hear? *[He laughs softly]* It is so quiet.

WIFE: What is the difference? Noise, quiet. *Noise, quiet.* It is all the same to me. —Do you think that I care? I am thinking of the cupboards and what is *in* them. —And what is *not* in them.

JUDGE: If only we had music.

        [The jury box bursts open. The JURY *are more formally arranged, as a chamber ensemble]*

JURY: Gosh golly me, why didn't you say so?
        We've been holding our breath waiting.
        Absolutely on our tippy toes.

        [One of them taps time with a bow. They play, always badly, something vaguely modern, e.g. Schoenberg, Bartok, beginning softly and nearly blaring by the end of the scene. The JUDGE *and his* WIFE *raise their voices correspondingly]*

WIFE: Why don't they play Wagner?

JUDGE: He's dead, my dear, long since dead. Is your left breast . . . *ready* for me now, hmmm?

WIFE: Ilke has the mumps.

JUDGE: Ah, youth. How far away it all seems.

WIFE: She is becoming sexually aware.

JUDGE: Do you remember that fall when I chased you through the rustling goldenrod?

WIFE: Yes. I had hay fever. I sneezed a lot. *[She laughs]* Yes, I sneezed a lot.

JUDGE: We were so giddy. The world was before us.

WIFE: *[Passionately] We shopped for crockery.*

JUDGE: What fat legs you had.

WIFE: Are you *erect*?

JUDGE: Not yet, not yet, my dear.

SON: *[Pounding]* Papa! Papa!

WIFE: Sometimes, husband, I thought you were a swine.

JUDGE: Wine? Yes, we should have wine.

> *[Almost instantaneously the ensemble leader snaps his fingers and one of the* JURY *comes out with a tray, wine, and two glasses. The* JUDGE *sips. His* WIFE *drinks it down in a gulp, laughs, and holds out her glass for more]*

I am so fond of May wine. Remember the *Schnaukenhaben* the first year we met? The bouquet? The transparency?

WIFE: *[Laughing now with drink]* What a fool you were.

JUDGE: I pulled up your skirts.

WIFE: *[Laughing]* And I pulled them down.

JUDGE: I pulled them up again.

WIFE: And I pulled them down again.

JUDGE: I chased you everywhere.

WIFE: *[Laughing]* What crockery we had! *[Holding him close]* Tell me about your case.

JUDGE: *[Embracing her]* It is very strange.

DAUGHTER: *[Pounding]* Papa! Papa! We are suffocating! I have found what is in my pants!

WIFE: *[To JUDGE]* What? I cannot hear you. Are you speaking?

JUDGE: It is a strange case. A strange crime.

WIFE: What is the accused like?

JUDGE: What? What did you say?

WIFE: Quick! Mount! . . . *Mount!* You must mount this very moment! I command you—mount! *[He rolls over on her]* Now push!

JUDGE: What?

WIFE: PUSH! *[She laughs] Puschen, mein kleine putzicle.*
[The JUDGE pushes, the knocking and pounding resume, the wine server dances classical ballet]

JUDGE: Nadia, you are so beautiful!

WIFE: PUSH!

JUDGE: I shall give you shelves of new crockery!

WIFE: *[Screaming]* PUSH!

JUDGE: How I loved to walk behind you!
  [She slaps his back vigorously as a signal to stop. He does not]

WIFE: *What is the crime? What is the crime?*

JUDGE: Crime? *Crime?* —Nadia, I feel guilty about your mother!

WIFE: *[Climactically]* Ahhhhh! —It doesn't matter. Roll over now! OFF!
  [A loud buzzer. Everything stops. The JURY *stares wide-eyed and open-mouthed]*

JUDGE: I must go, Nadia.

WIFE: *[Angrily]* But you have just come!

JUDGE: But you heard—

WIFE: Oh, go, go. Go, come. Go, *come.* What is the difference when the crockery is all cracked?

JUDGE: But why haven't you told me this before?
  [Buzzer. Sudden blackout. Then lights up in the courtroom]
  [To ATTENDANT*]* Who, pray tell, is the next witness?

ATTENDANT: His Excellency, the Water Commissioner.

JUDGE: *[Still dressing]* His excellency. My, my, my. Is that higher than His Honor? —Why is it so dark?

ATTENDANTS: *[Mumbling]* Hear, hear . . . .

ATTENDANT: *[Confidentially]* He is said to be quite a dish.

JURY: Well, for heaven's sake, dish him up then.
  I'm exhausted.

JUDGE: *[Oratorically]* I am quite relaxed. Quite. *[Aside]* —But I don't really believe it, do I? *[He laughs]*

ATTENDANT: The Court calls his Excellency, the Water Commissioner, to the witness stand.

> *[Pause. Commotion. Anticipation. The* WATER COMMISSIONER *comes from the* AUDIENCE *or lobby. He is gorgeously, ornately, but nevertheless dowdily, attired in black. A rich dowager, a musty drag-queen. Heavily and clumsily made up. He is the* JEW *of earlier]*

WATER COMMISSIONER: *[Bustling forward]* Oi, I thought you'd never call me . . . . I've been turning taps off all over town. You'd never *believe* the leaky faucets in this metropolis. Drip, drip, drip everywhere. *[To someone in the* AUDIENCE*]* Hello, darling . . . . Excuse me, please . . . . Watch my gown, *sir* . . . . No, you may *not* have my private number. *[He laughs]* They simply don't make washers the way they used to. The golden age of plumbing is definitely past. We're all leaking down the drain . . . . *[Reaching the witness stand]* There. At last. *[He sits with a heavy sigh and arranges his wardrobe]* I do believe in civic duty. I was raised to believe in civic duty. So here I am.

JURY: *[During and/or after his mini-processional]*
Ooooh-la-la.
What a frump.
Diversion at last.
[Melodramatically] Alas, mine sight is struck a sudden blow!

WATER COMMISSIONER: I *heard* that, young *person.*

> *[The* JURY *laughs]*

JUDGE: *[To* ATTENDANT, *irritably]* Open the blinds more. Let in more light.

ATTENDANTS: *[Mumbling]* Hear, hear . . . .

JURY: About time.

JUDGE: —My god, how relaxed I am! *[He looks about nervously]*

WATER COMMISSIONER: Oh, so am I, so am I. Like a good, thorough flush.

JURY: What romantic imagery.
It goes with the outfit, dear.
[The WATER COMMISSIONER *laughs shrilly]*

ATTENDANT: Do you swear—

WATER COMMISSIONER: Never. *[He laughs shrilly]*

JUDGE: *[Irritably]* Will the witness kindly stop laughing— *[Suddenly polite]* so we may proceed—

WATER COMMISSIONER: With what, dearie? *[He laughs shrilly again]* Do you know I have a marvelous collection of *plungers*? With one of them I can actually abort—

JURY: What a gross imagination.

WATER COMMISSIONER: I adore grossness. It's like mother's milk to me.
[Laughs]

JUDGE: Milk? Did the witness say milk?

JURY: Wonderful. The plunger that aborts is like mother's milk to her.
[They laugh]
Tell us about your job, Aunty.

> *[The* WATER COMMISSIONER *looks at the* JUDGE, *then at the* DEFENSE *and* PROSECUTION, *all of whom look at each other]*

WATER COMMISSIONER: Do you mean it? Talk about my job? It just so happens that I *love* to talk about my job. By the way, I have only limited time. We're cutting a ribbon in a new urinal today and—

JURY: *[Clapping]* Hear, hear.
Bravo.
Do have your plunger ready.
Yes, and—

WATER COMMISSIONER: *[Pettishly]* Let me get on with my number, will you? What a fiendish collection you are. *[They laugh]* —Where was I? Oh, yes. And I'm cutting a spot for TV. Water Protection Week, you know. Hmmm? . . . . *Well.* Mondays I always leave free for sewer inspection. I have a special outfit I wear. You wouldn't believe the Monday sewers. Lots and lots of good lumber. The pigeons are getting in there and scavenging like sea gulls. The rats make six foot leaps, very graceful really, grab them in mid-flight, and swim away to their lairs. If that's what rats have. Lairs, I mean. Do you know those little creatures can actually *tread water?* —Can you believe it? *[Pause]* I have a special barge with lights, and I sit on a poop deck, gorgeously arrayed. They know me so well down there. How grandly do I float o'er the miasmic way. With a chorus of squeaks. And I think I can tell you that *all is going well.* No dramatic changes in the effluences. Air pressure uniform. And a *high* level of wonderment. *[Pause]* Do you want more? *[Silence]* What particular day do you want? *[Silence. Everyone is staring at him]* —Do you mind if I rehearse my number? —It's a dilly. —Could I have music, girls?

[He gets down from the witness stand, sings a note for pitch, then a song and dance number]

> Beware,
> Your water may be poisoned.
> Beware,
> Your water may be foul.
> A rat
> Lies stinking in the basement,
> And can-
> Cer lies in wait for you.

JURY: Utterly charming.
        A Chopinesque flavor.

WATER COMMISSIONER: Do you really like it? I wrote it myself. —Then I say, *[Formally]* "This is your Water Commissioner warning you that your next drink may kill you, or at least make you very sick. *[He smiles brightly for the camera fade-out, then abruptly laughs and takes the stand again]* Well? Dance, anyone? Mustard? *[No one speaks. With menace] All right then. [He puts his shawl over his head and becomes a sinister crone and speaks raspingly] Lies! All lies! Political obfuscation* Obviously you want to know about *the deeper levels.* Everyone wants to know about the deeper levels. Where does it all go? How much headroom is there left? Do I need face mask and flippers to inspect? What is the *scum* content? Oh, yes, I've

seen the defendant. Listen. Fridays, just for example, I am a free agent.
I go where the plumbing takes me. And I tell you the pipes are corroded.
They are clogged. If they do not burst, it will all back up. *Back up.* Fetuses,
turds, and orange peels stinking in your sink. What will you do with it?
It will fill all your houses, your institutions. Half blind pigeons will fly the
streets and avenues aiming for your eyes. You will be buried softly with
small feet treading on your heads. Get out your plungers! Clear the
drains! Get your snakes into the pipes! Scrape, ream, blow air! It's all
backing up, backing up! Nothing is clean but the shit itself! Use your
noses! Smell! Smell and vomit! I am warning you. *[Squawking, laughing,
and flapping like a diseased cock as he leaves]* Pawk! PAWK! PAWK!
PAWK! . . .

JURY: Ping.
          That was a bad one.
          Ping.
          Definitely shiver town.
          Ping.
          Sounds to me like a sinus problem.
          Ping.
          Do turn up the heat.

                    [The JUDGE *gavels]*

JUDGE: Recess!

ATTENDANT: Recess!

PROSECUTION and DEFENSE: Objection! . . .

JUDGE: Stained! —More light! More light! Air!

ATTENDANTS: *[Mumbling]* Hear, hear . . . .

                    [Lights immediately out. A spot on the JUDGE's *bed, in
                    which his* WIFE *and* CHILDREN*]*

WIFE: Husband? Husband?

JUDGE: *[Off]* Coming. Coming. *[Entering]* Ah, thank god, what a domestic
scene. What a haven. And the children, too.

SON: Papa. Why did you keep us in the closet? We could have died.

DAUGHTER: Papa. What will become of me? How do I become pregnant? Why are you always boiling water? And in so large a kettle?

SON: Papa. I would like a pony of two colors. And when I'm grown up, a horse. Also of two colors. Why don't you read to me any more? Where are my fairy tales?

DAUGHTER: Papa. I am becoming distraught. I am afraid of you.

SON: Papa. Your belly is soft. Your pu-pu has a bad smell.

JUDGE: *[Laughing]* Children, children—

WIFE: It is no laughing matter, Klaus.

JUDGE: *[Moved]* Klaus. Do you know how many years it has been since you used my name?

SON: Are you really Klaus, Papa? Were you Klaus when you made me?

JUDGE: *[Laughing]* Listen to the little rascal.

DAUGHTER: It is an ungainly name. It opens the mouth too wide. Look. *Klaus. Klaus.*

JUDGE: And why not—*[Slowly emphasizing]* Ilka? *[He laughs]*

DAUGHTER: Don't call me that. Call me daughter. You don't care what happens to me. I shall be ravished.

WIFE: Come to bed. You look silly standing there.
       [He enters the bed]
Your shoes!
       [He takes off his shoes and lies down, the CHILDREN *between him and his* WIFE*]*

JUDGE: Ah, this is so relaxing. *[He reaches across to touch his* WIFE*]* Isn't it relaxing, Nadia?

WIFE: No. It is not relaxing. I do not find it relaxing.

JUDGE: Here we are all four, cozy and warm. *Snug.* On a good mattress, a solid bed. All the troubles of the world at bay.

SON: Papa. I hear them howling.

JUDGE: Hear what, my son?

SON: The troubles. *[He howls]*

JUDGE: *[Laughing]* Do you hear him, Nadia? What an imagination he has. He will be a poet.

WIFE: He will be dead.

JUDGE: What? How can you say such a horrible thing? This is monstrous.

SON: Papa. What is my name? Am I Klaus, Jr.? —I am being sucked away. I feel it. Hold me, Papa.

> *[The* JUDGE *laughs]*

WIFE: You haven't said anything about the crockery. Have you been thinking about the crockery?

JUDGE: I think about it all the time. It never leaves my brain. —Even when I make love, Nadia, I think of the crockery.

WIFE: That makes me very happy.

DAUGHTER: *[To the* JUDGE*]* You should speak only what is fit for my ears.

SON: *[Taking a knife from under the pillow]* Papa. What is this? I found it under your pillow?

JUDGE: It is always under my pillow. *[Snatching it]* Give it to me.

SON: Papa. You frighten me. I do not *like* the name of Klaus.

JUDGE: *[Putting the knife to his* SON*'s throat]* So, I frighten you. Would you like to be a judge, like me?

SON: I don't know what a judge does, Papa. Will you take the knife away? Can I change my name when I am grown up?

DAUGHTER: For shame, Papa.

JUDGE: *[Laughing]* Do you hear them, Nadia? For shame. Change his name.

WIFE: Oh, slit and be done. The roast will burn.

JUDGE: Son, I judge. I condemn people. *I mete out justice.*

SON: Ahh, I am glad you have told me, Papa. Now *I* can tell my *teacher.* He will—

   [The JUDGE's DAUGHTER *clutches her stomach and groans loudly]*

DAUGHTER: What is this pain I feel! What is this pain! Tell me, Papa. Kiss me! Be passionate!

JUDGE: What pain? You are only seventeen!
    [She groans again. A buzzer]
   I must go. Duty calls me. I have a difficult case to settle.

WIFE: *I am warning you. Think about the crockery.*

JUDGE: Can we dance?

   [His DAUGHTER *groans]*

SON: Papa—

   [Lights out, then up. The Court is in session]

JUDGE: *[Dressing]* Is the Defense ready for the summing up?

JURY: Summing up?
   Great heavenly savior, we've hardly begun. —Have we?
   Hardly, indeed.

Words, words.

JUDGE: The bench is willing to dispense with the formal middle. The bench despises the grayness of the day. The bench—

[The DEFENSE *pirouettes and bows flamboyantly]*

DEFENSE: We are ready, Your Honor. Gladly and without respite. The end above all.

JURY: This is becoming *gorgeous.*
          In the law, courtesy is everything.
          What a glorious hallmark.
          I feel like singing. *[He or she does, operatically]*

[The DEFENSE, PROSECUTION, *and their* ASSISTANTS *join in]*

[Screaming] I do believe it's the *party* at last! I must dance! *[He begins to climb out of the jury box]* Oh, happy, happy, hap—

[The JUDGE *gavels]*

JUDGE: By god, you are stirring me up again. *Ladies and gentlemen. — Must I always suffer? Why am I confused?*

PROSECUTION: *[Rushing to the* JURY*]* You must hang this man!

JURY: That's all?
          No frills?
          How *bold, bad,* and *bald.*

DEFENSE: Oh, never! *Never!* This man is innocent!

PROSECUTOR: *[Tap-dancing backwards quickly]* The bones do not lie!

JURY: Of course. Bones *lay. You* lie. *[Giggles]*

PROSECUTOR: You have been told how he was caught red-handed.

JURY: *Red-handed?* Was it that bad?
          A mere bucket of paint.

Was he actually caught? I must have missed something.
My dear, you miss *every*thing.
Gaaaaa.

DEFENSE: *[After a few gracious turns]* Dear, dear jury, you may take *my* word for it, his hands, if anything, were *chartreuse.* And what does that mean?

JURY: I wouldn't dare say, I'm sure.
Do tell us.

DEFENSE: Precisely. And thank you. *[He blows a kiss]* On the night in question, there was a *half* moon. Ponder. Yes, ponder. The accused had eaten a full meal and stroked his cat Minnie. Ponder again. Stroked her fourteen times. Ponder well.
[Pause]

JURY: The sound of pondering.
Ah.
Wonder of Allah.
A *Minnie!*
   [The PROSECUTOR *works up a fast tap step, which he concludes in front of the* JURY. *They clap politely]*
Oh, bravo.
Well done.
I have never seen the fish with two cucumbers executed so well.
He must have a heart of gold.

PROSECUTOR: *[In heavy Germanic]* Ah, so. Gold, huh. You are calling me a heart of gold. *Gut. Gut.* I will accept your heart of gold. *[He nods and clicks his heels]* So, now. We go to the business, huh? Defense says accused is innocent. *But . . .* does mother of accused say innocent? —No. How are we to know this fact? Because I am telling you it. Give me your look now. Is it crooked? What is this Shinbone Alley, huh? I do not lie. Accused is like *schmutz.* His arm he is raising in anger. For please, help me, he says, I am a lost one. *[He laughs contemptuously]* How is he a lost? I will now tell you. He is *not* a lost one. He is a lazy and fat in his head. For this man, will you let live, I ask? Excusing me passion. I am, in my *being,* on the section, the *midriff,* of justice. Hear me, juries of men and womans. Kill this man a menace before he is worse. Is no doubt. No doubt. Cut into his throat *at once!* Yes?

*[He clicks his heels and nods, does a quick tap step backwards
to wild applause from his table, as the* JUDGE *gavels them to
silence]*

JURY:　His charm is overwhelming, don't you think?
　　　　And I love his stiff upper lip.
　　　　A definite boon to society.
　　　　Oh, what's this?

　　　　[The DEFENSE *is performing some flowing ballet turns and
　　　　leaps. He ends kneeling before the* JURY, *who clap politely, etc.]*

DEFENSE:　Hear *me*, oh men and women of honor!

JURY:　You've got my number, my man.

DEFENSE:　The small bird flits from blossom to blossom. The bees their
nectar take. And babbles the brook 'neath airy skies.

JURY:　Oh, toothsome, toothsome.
　　　　And a dilly-dum-down-o.

DEFENSE:　My heart aches for the woe of man. Beset by life. Lost from his
Maker.

JURY:　Oh, true, Mr. Defense, true.
　　　　But also horseshit, don't you think? With a sprig of holly, of
course.

DEFENSE:　Prickled by a thousand conflicting anxieties, temptations,
hates, passions—

JURY:　Fignewtons.
　　　　Constipation.
　　　　And terrible, terrible sales help.

DEFENSE:　The Prosecutor says *Shinebone Alley.* And *I* say, *What of that?
What of that?* To Shinbone Alley I oppose—*corn flowers.*

JURY:　Make it azaleas and I'll buy it.

DEFENSE:　Walk through our cemeteries. *Read* the inscriptions for the
living.

JURY: On the head
I once was hit,
And now lie here,
A pile of shit.
[They laugh uproariously]

DEFENSE: *Feel* the beckoning finger. My friends, we sink down. We all sink down, clutching, grasping, for the blue blossoms, which cannot hold us. And when we are gone, only the scattered, broken, *dying* clusters of petal, fragrant *clots* of what once we were, of what once we sought to grasp, to hold, forever. But, ladies and gentlemen, we cannot. The flowers are fleeting for us. A brief smell, a vision of loveliness—

JURY: *[In imitation]* Like the swift look beneath the billowing summer frock.

DEFENSE: —and no more. That, *that*, is life, my friends. Small as it is, do not take it from the accused.
[He dances eloquently backwards on his toes. Abrupt cheers, etc.]

JURY: *[Several of whom cry in each other's arms]*
Bravo.
Oh, bravo.
[Dabbing eyes] Heart warming and heart rending.
I could have peed in my pants.

JUDGE: *[Gaveling]* Ladies and gentlemen of the jury, *time, time!* *[Pointing to the window]* Look!

ATTENDANTS: *[Mumbling]* Hear, hear . . . .

JUDGE: You have heard the evidence, you have heard the argument of the Defense and the Prosecution. The crockery is now up to—

[Gasps]

JURY: *[ALL]*
WHAT?
[Pause. Freeze. The JUDGE giggles at his gaffe. Lights out suddenly. Then up on his home. His WIFE is slowly breaking crockery, a piece at a time]

JUDGE: Nadia! Nadia! What do you do?

WIFE: *[Angrily]* There was no milk today!

JUDGE: Forget the milk! *I* will get you milk! *[She continues to break the crockery]* Nadia! Stop! This is insane!

[She laughs]

WIFE: I warned you, Helmut!

JUDGE: *Helmut?* I am not *Helmut.*

WIFE: *[Pausing]* Not *Helmut?* Where is your knife?

JUDGE: *Where are the children?*

WIFE: I do not know any *Helmut.*

JUDGE: *[Frenzied] Where are the children?*

WIFE: Why are you talking to me? Have you come to clean the windows? *[She laughs. The* JUDGE *searches frantically for the knife]* You have been sleeping in my bed these twenty years and you are not *Helmut?* Is it possible you are a swine?

JUDGE: *[Finding the knife]* Ahh, here is the knife. Perhaps I am *Helmut* after all? *[He laughs]* Helmut with the milk?

WIFE: Perhaps you will kill me also?

JUDGE: *[Stepping towards her slowly]* Today I am concluding my most difficult case.

WIFE: Slit me from ear to ear? The house is spic and span.

JUDGE: *[Nearer]* And when I will judge—

WIFE: Yes?

JUDGE: *[Nearer]* —after—

WIFE: Yes?

JUDGE: *[Nearer] —all chaos is come.*

WIFE: Chaos?

JUDGE: *[Nearer] Yes.*

WIFE: What is this *chaos*? What will we do? Will we—

JUDGE: *[Holding the knife towards her and laughing]* Can you guess?

WIFE: You mean?—

JUDGE: *Yes. Say it.*

WIFE: Buy—

TOGETHER: *Crockery!*
          [They laugh. Pounding. A loud buzzer]

CHILDREN: Papa! Papa! . . .

WIFE: Husband, you are such a goose.

JUDGE: Nadia. I love the embrace of your woman's body.

WIFE: *[Feeling her body problematically but sensually]* But—

          [Pounding, loud buzzer]

CHILDREN: Papa! Papa! . . .

JUDGE: But—

          [Pounding, loud buzzer. His WIFE *slowly picks up a dish and
          drops it. It breaks. She laughs in a low, sensual voice, slowly
          picks up another dish, is about to drop it. Loud buzzer. Lights
          out, then up on the Court]*

JURY: Despicable.
       I really think this calls for a cry of rage.

Be my guest, darling.
> *[He or she screams. Others scream. Silence]*

My god.
I feel much better.
I'm not sure it was really rage.
Close enough, dear. Close enough.
> *[They play a sloppy musical chord]*

JUDGE: *[Disoriented]* Er ... ladies and gentlemen of the jury—I beg you—
I—

JURY: You see. I *told* you I was a lady.

DEFENSE: We object to anything you might say, Your Honor.

PROSECUTION: Sustained!

> *[The* JURY *giggles. The* ASSISTANTS *politely applaud. The* JUDGE *gavels]*

JUDGE: As you can see, the case is a difficult one. The hour—

ATTENDANTS: Hear, hear . . . .

JUDGE: On the one hand, you must determine whether or not the defendant, who has not testified—

JURY: Oh, has he not!

JUDGE: —is worthy of your respect. And on the other hand, can you believe the testimony of the witness, to wit—

JURY: Oh, do skip it.

JUDGE: *[Forging on]* In this particular case, it is important to remember that the status *in quo situ* is not a factor. *[Pause]* On the other hand, perhaps it is a factor. Nor can you consider the broad range of deformity. Time, however, being constant, is a factor. The alleged crime was in fact— note this, please—perpetrated at a given time. But *what* time exactly? And by whom? By whom?

JURY: Surely he isn't asking us? Teeny-weeny us?

JUDGE: That is for you to determine. That is your task. *How* seems not to be much in question. A throat was put to a sharpened blade and a life was extinguished.

JURY: How quaint.
Yes. Quaintly put.

JUDGE: But which life? *[Pause]* —There is some question here. It has been made clear that you are to disregard entirely the area—

JURY: Area? Doesn't he mean jurisdiction?

JUDGE: —of motive. It is altogether too murky. Dark, if you like. —Yes, *dark.* —Oh, my god!

ATTENDANTS: *[Mumbling]* Hear, hear . . . .

JURY: Ahh, dark. *Now* we're getting to the heart of the matter.
The pit, dear, the pit.

JUDGE: Compassion likewise cannot be . . . a consideration?

JURY: But is it a *factor*?
And what about *hearsay*? We *always* have *hearsay*.

JUDGE: Now, the *idea* that the victim was young—

DEFENSE: Old!

JUDGE: Attractive.

DEFENSE: Ugly!

JUDGE: Healthy.

DEFENSE: Diseased!

JUDGE: Should not, let us say, lead you to . . . interpolate—

JURY: I *love* interpolate.

JUDGE: —factors—

JURY: *Again.*

JUDGE: —that might lead to unwarranted—

JURY: Oh, dear.

JUDGE: —qualifications—

JURY: I *never* leave my apartment without a qualification.

JUDGE: —of challengeable—

JURY: Honor above all!

JUDGE: —substance.

JURY: Is that ultimate or *pen*ultimate?
What a mouthful of turd.
As if we knew.
And how gauche.
  [They laugh and begin, one by one, to take out their instruments and tune them]
Should we ask him a question?
Verboten.
Ist it really, darling?
Yah, you *crapenzeit.*
Coquette.

JUDGE: The jury must remember—

JURY: Cut it!

JUDGE: I beg your pardon?

JURY: Cut it!
Snip!
Snip!
And *snap*, you dog!

JUDGE: But—

JURY: *[Shrilly, several]*

The crockery! . . .
The crockery, Judgie! . . .

JUDGE: *[Rising]* What? What? But— You dare to— You have the— You cannot— Nadia! Nadia! *[Frantically, as he steps down]* NADIA!

> *[Lights out, then up immediately on the JUDGE's home. Meal time]*

WIFE: What did the doctor say, husband?

JUDGE: What doctor? I haven't seen a doctor.

WIFE: Do you have cancer or not?

SON: Papa. My teacher said we all have cancer.

JUDGE: What nonsense is this? Why are you saying this? *Nadia.* Account for this. I have come home for lunch. *Lunch.*

WIFE: Isn't that how it happens, husband? You come home for lunch, a few minutes late, and suddenly—

SON: You can't pee, Papa, you can't pee.

JUDGE: What? Are you mad? You are killing me already? I tell you I haven't *seen* any doctor.

WIFE: Husband, what good would it do? We have mushroom and barley soup.

JURY: *[Whispering loudly]*
Cancer.
Cancer.
Cancer . . . .

JUDGE: Ohh, mushroom and barley soup. On a cold day. My family all around. Memories of my mother.

DAUGHTER: And prostate, Papa. Prostate.

SON: Some people get it on the tips of their noses, Papa. It's because of where they smell.

JUDGE: Smell?

JURY: *[Whispering loudly]*
Cancer . . . .

JUDGE: Stop it! Stop it! This is my *home. [To* SON*] You* sound vulgar. *[To* DAUGHTER*]* I'm *ashamed* of you.

CHILDREN: We love you, Papa.

JUDGE: *[Relenting, smiling]* How can I resist you? Mushroom and barley soup. How I can smell it. And cucumbers, radishes, onions, and sour cream. Nadia, I always thought of you as *a bowl of sour cream.* —Nadia. *[Eating] I eat the sour cream!*

WIFE: *[Coyly]* Tsk. The children will hear you, Klaus.

JUDGE: *[Expansively]* Let them. Let them. It is time they learned about life.

DAUGHTER: Yes, Papa, it *is* time. I agree with what you say. Am I like sour cream yet, Papa?

JUDGE: *[Laughing]* Do you hear, Nadia? What a frisky, sassy lassy she is?

SON: Papa. Look. *[Stuffing his mouth with sour cream]* I eat the sour cream!

WIFE: I don't think it is right, husband.

SON: I don't *like* the sour cream, Papa!

JUDGE: Son, Vienna was *built* on sour cream.

SON: Papa. We don't live in Vienna!

JUDGE: Oh, what does it matter? We live *here, today,* and we have mushroom and barley soup. *[He cries suddenly, takes his* WIFE's *hand]* Oh, Nadia, my mother would have been so happy to be here!

WIFE: You are being mawkish. Your mother is—

SON: Eat your soup, Papa. It will get cold.

JUDGE: Yes. Yes. Eat my soup. What else can I do, my dears, but eat my soup?
>   *[They begin eating the soup, slowly but noisily]*

DAUGHTER: Faster, Papa.
>   *[The* JUDGE *eats faster]*

SON: More, Papa. More. I hear them again. *[He howls]*

>   *[The* JUDGE *slobbers his soup in haste]*

WIFE: Hurry, husband, *hurry.*

>   *[The* JUDGE *drops his spoon, puts his face in the bowl, and sucks. His* WIFE *and* CHILDREN *laugh at him. A loud buzzer]*

JUDGE: *[His face in the bowl]* I cannot eat any faster! *[The buzzer again. He lifts his head]* Am I late? Am I too late?

>   *[He stares at them. His* SON *runs and puts on the tango record. His* DAUGHTER *stands abruptly. They swiftly take a ready position, poise, then dance—formally but intensely. His* SON *and* WIFE *take positions in the same way and join them. Loud buzzer. Courtroom noise and activity pick up. They keep dancing. Loud buzzer. They stop. Loud* JURY *laughter, drowning out music. Lights out, then up on court-room]*

JURY: And how is your cancer today, darling?
Cancer never bothers me. Cancer is a metaphor.
How droll.
I remember well a cancer of my youth. It—
Oh, eat it and shut up.
Oh, I did, I did. But it didn't shut me up.

Nothing, I fear, will *ever* shut you up, my dear.
It's my amazing vitality. *[Mocking] Oh, Nadia, I love the sexual embrace.* —Didn't you love that line?

[The JUDGE gavels. Silence]

JUDGE: *[Somewhat bewildered. Dishevelled and tired]* The court . . .
offers an apology. . . . The court is tired . . . . The court cannot keep track
of time any longer. . . .

ATTENDANTS: Hear, hear. . . .

JUDGE: It appears . . . outside . . . to be . . . The court— *[Snapping out of his mood, straightening his robes, wig, grandiloquently but clearly an effort, forced] The case of the cock that crew.*
             [A Chord]

JURY: A divertimento oblongato.
           A mudulla oblongata.
           A pudenda obligata.
           I'm thrilled and convinced it will be fascinating.
           Uplifting.
           Just possibly edifying.
           But isn't it a bit late? We've already been here for—
           Ever. Amen.

JUDGE: Whether 'tis right in everything aforesaid to judge quickly and
punish expeditiously or whether to stand back and look beneath the lay
of— I don't know what I'm saying. *[He giggles] I don't know what I'm saying. [He giggles]*

JURY: Of course not, darling.
           How clever of you to see.

JUDGE: —things for what may truer be. Do we rest, or do we turn? . . .
Burn? *[He giggles again]* Which road? *[And again]* And for whatever
itches ail us, what balm by the wayside . . . do we . . . *endure?*

JURY: *[The SILLY, clapping]* Hear, hear. Hear, hear.
             [Someone slaps his head with a fan]

JUDGE: Oh, almighty god. Creator. Bless— *[He giggles]*

JURY: Piss on.
        [Another swat]

JUDGE: —These proceedings. Give wisdom—
        [Taps of approval from the JURY*]*
        —where we hesitate . . . *[Laughing]* in the dark road of—of—

JURY: *[The* SILLY*] Justice*, you silly *man*.
        [Approbation from the others]

JUDGE: And— And—
        [His WIFE *screams off stage]*

WIFE: *[Off]* Husband! Husband! Come quick!

> *[Lights out, then up on the* JUDGE's *home. He runs in. No one is there. He looks around, sees the knife and picks it up. Pounding. His* WIFE *screams again. He turns abruptly and looks at the* AUDIENCE, *then at the knife. Lights out]*

SON and DAUGHTER: *Papa! Papa!* . . . *[They scream. Sounds of violent deaths]*

> *[Lights up on courtroom]*

DEFENSE, PROSECUTION, and ASSISTANTS: *[Milling about]* Object! Foul! We object! Unfair! Objection! . . .

JUDGE: *[Rushing to the bench]* I'm coming! I'm coming! *[He gavels. They sit]* There. There, now. Where were we? *[He clears his throat]* Ahh. The jury must remember—

JURY: *[Shrilly]*
        The crockery?
        What about the crockery?

JUDGE: But we just— You cannot— I—

> *[A brief vision of the bloodied and dead children]*

DEFENSE, PROSECUTION, and ASSISTANTS: We object! We cannot abide this! Intolerable!

JUDGE: What? New evidence? We cannot allow new evidence. The testimony is all in. I cannot *deal* with new evidence.

ASSISTANTS: Objection! Objection!

JUDGE: *[Wildly]* Sustained! Sustained! I sustain everything!

JURY: *[Shrilly]*
There's always new evidence!
What about the knife under your pillow?
What about the knife under your pillow?

ASSISTANTS: Objection! Objection! . . .

JUDGE: Sustained! They are sustained, I tell you! —What knife! How dare you ask me? *[To* ATTENDANT*]* What time is it?

ATTENDANTS: *[Mumbling]* Hear, hear. . . .

JURY: *[Shrilly]*
Why don't you have milk in your coffee, dear?
        [They laugh]
There are clean socks in your drawer.
        [They laugh]

DEFENSE: Objection!

PROSECUTION: Outrageous!

DEFENSE: Anarchy!

JURY: Do you think we could set this to music?
        [They begin to play, but haphazzardly]
And Judge, darling, why are your windows so dirty?
        [They laugh]

JUDGE: *[Beside himself]* They are not dirty! They are clean! Very clean! *[To himself]* But why are they so clean? *[To the court]* You swine! Why should they not be dirty? What is there to look at? The streets? The people? They have taken away the park! The animals in the zoo are dead! Dead, do you hear? Maggots will fill the cages. The children suck their bones. For *what*, for *what*?

JURY: *[Mockingly]*
Crockery!
Crockery!
Crockery!

JUDGE: *[Furious]* You swine! You are all swine!

DEFENSE: Your Honor—

PROSECUTOR: Your Honor—

TOGETHER: This is a mistrial.

JUDGE: You swine! This is my *life*!
[One of the JURY *taps a wine glass musically]*
Swine!
[He taps again]
Swine!
[The JUDGE *takes the bloody knife and rushes toward the* JURY*]*

JURY: Oh, dear, we're in for it now.

[Freeze. Blackout. Lights up on the JUDGE'S *home. His* WIFE *is standing, looking out the window. The* JUDGE *enters with the bloodied knife]*

WIFE: I cannot see a thing. Once I could see. Now, it is all . . . *gray.* Everything is gray.

JUDGE: Nadia.

WIFE: Why have you deceived me?

JUDGE: *I*? I only loved you.

WIFE: Loved? You wore your robes to bed.

JUDGE: Nadia. I am a judge.

WIFE: You are a fool. —Where are the children?

JUDGE: —Dead. They were too . . . limp. I . . . slit their throats.

WIFE: *You . . . slit . . . their. . . .*

JUDGE: From ear to— What else could I— *What was there to live for? Nadia!* Hear me! —I am a judge! I *judge!*

JURY: *[Laughing]*
        Hear him.
        Rich.
        Just like a minstrel show.
        Give us a mammy, Judge.

JUDGE: Nadia. I want to make love.
                [She turns and drops a dish. It breaks]
        We can make more. We can make more. We *must. Nadia.*
                [She slowly opens her robe to him. He approaches slowly,
holding the knife]
        We can make more! We can make more! *Tomorrow and tomor-*
row. . . .
                [She encloses him and the knife. Convulsions]
        Nadia!

WIFE: *[Sobbing]* Husband! Husband! Husband! We are old! So old!

JUDGE: Young! We are young! *[Rhapsodically]* Hollyhocks! Sleeves of gold! —And we can dance, Nadia! *Dance!* Do you hear?

WIFE: Then let us dance! *God, let us dance!*

                [Tango music. Tightly clasped, they dance. Gradually every-
                one in the courtroom joins in. It becomes an exit procession]

JUDGE: *[Cutting everything short]* Wait! *Wait!* Do you hear it? Shhhh! Listen!

                [As the lights dim, the cock begins to crow, gradually becom-

*ing louder until it dominates and becomes a hair-raising
sound]*

ALL: *[Through the crowing]*
Vive la justice!
Vive la justice!
Vive la justice!

*[Lights out. Then, when they go on again, entire cast on stage.
The* JUDGE *silences the* AUDIENCE, *steps forward and delivers
the epilog]*

EPILOG

Well, now. Here we are, where we began,
Having covered a two hour span.
The world turns round, and on its toes
Dances Spanish fandangos,
Sings a song, mutters twice,
Once for fire, once for ice.
Go, now. Fill your bellies with drink,
And perhaps, just once, take pause to think:
Justice is done; you can see I mean it;
So do get out your rags—and clean it.

*[He steps back and smiles. They all bow. Tango music as
lights go down and out]*

END

SOME PRODUCTION NOTES ON *La Justice*
BY THE AUTHOR

La Justice is built on two contrasting ideas: order and disintegration. On the one hand, there is the structure of the court with its implications of law, order, logic, a firm sense of right and wrong, even omniscience, and ultimately justice, something we all want in life. The judge, like the detective in the classic mystery, is faced with a disruption in the social order. Just as the detective, through the application of rationality, finds the criminal and restores a sense of order, so too does the judge, through the organization of the court, punish the guilty, redress wrongs, etc. Our sense of well being and safety in society depends in great part on our faith in the efficacy of the courts, particularly in their function of meting out justice. We can also say that our confidence in the actuality of societal justice is parallel to a more amorphous confidence in the actuality of divine justice: we have a deep need to believe that at the root of things there *is* a balance struck, that things are set right, etc.

But how reliable *is* any concept or sense of justice? How secure are we really, in society, in life, in the world? What, or where, really, is justice? What is the "justice" of the human condition? Two things are possibly on trial here: justice itself and that divine judge who has meted out the "justice" of the human condition, i.e. god himself.

The judge in *La Justice* initially takes comfort in the forms and paraphernalia of court life—the ritual and pomp, the stylization, the rhetoric (e.g. *a fortiori, de facto*). But almost immediately it is apparent that he has doubt, reservation, anxiety. Things are not right. These intimations of disintegration are most focused in his concern with the passage of day to night, youth to age, spring to winter, and life to death. These concerns are the center of the second idea in the play, disintegration, the idea that foundations (the things we have taken for granted as certainties) are crumbling away. This idea is represented by, for example, the fading and cracked crockery, his wife's infidelity, the breakdown of his family life, his son's rotten teeth, the jury's "bleeding black hole," the pollution and decay revealed by the water commissioner Jew, disease and deformity (the cancer of the body, the body politic, and the soul), even his wife's name, Nadia (*Nada*).

In court he is faced with the empty (but not always meaningless) rhetoric of the defense and prosecution—travesties of the juridical method, an anarchic jury intent on its own pleasures and totally impervious to the hypocrisies and clichés of court life, a defendant who is not present, a witness who seems mysteriously involved in the corruption of his own family life, and a cock that will not crow (i.e. "justice" that will not reveal itself). His sense of security evaporates, his power and control evanesce. He turns in desperation to his island of domestic life for assurance and comfort, but even there the crockery is cracked, he cannot have his sex, his children alternately importune and mock. They would have him dying of cancer or cuckolded.

Straddling both areas, court and home, is the Jew—the survivor *par excellence*, the prince of disintegration. He can clean windows, deliver milk, he has Mexican numbers, Albanian numbers, he can sing, dance, imitate donkeys. No matter where you put him down, he is up again somewhere else: He survives. His survival capacity is explained by his role as water commissioner, a man who, floating on his miasmic barge like some hellish Cleopatra, *sees* the garbage, the corruption of his society, everything it would hide by flushing into the sewer. He survives because he knows the *whole* truth. And, apocalyptically, he issues a warning to those who would hear the truth instead of pretty platitudes: *stop, now, before it is too late. The world is turning into a huge shit pile.*

But the judge cannot *see.* As his wife says, he wears his robes to bed. He does not truly feel the human condition. He is a man of empty forms. And when the forms break down (under the force of this particular trial) he disintegrates. He sleeps with a knife under his pillow; he keeps water boiling for some devilish contingency; his thoughts turn to violence. He eats soup while society burns. He hears neither his wife nor children; the latter begin to fear him. He does not heed his son's perception of the jungle howls nor his daughter's sudden manifestation of the pain of (adult) life. He is, in fact, as blind as the pigeons flying in the dark sewers, whom voracious rats leap at and drag away to their lairs to devour.

As a final act of desperation and panic he kills his own children, his faith in the future. They were, he thinks, too flaccid. It all seems too hopeless, too hopeless.

But the play is not entirely without hope. The judge has periodically remembered his youthful love for Nadia, a time of spring and flowers, "uncracked crockery," a better world. Even Nadia and the children soften to his recollections. His final knife thrust to Nadia is both a culmination of the disintegrating impulse of the play, a final "death," but also a sexual thrust of renewal and life. Even when all seems gone, they have still each other, they are not yet "too old," time has not completely run out. They can begin again "tomorrow." And so they dance—tragically, painfully, and courageously. If they could not dance, there would indeed be nothing. This time round however, he's not the judge, he is the *man*. He is not blind and he has no blind faith in empty forms. He sees, suffers, and lives.

Miscellaneous

The frame: The play is framed by two prologues and an epilog to give some idea of the play's content but also to provide a formal elegance of structure parallel to the court structure to contrast with the chaos of disintegration within the play, to sharpen the poignancy and irony. It is also to provide an association with the age of heroic drama (e.g. Dryden, Rowe, Otway), an age of far greater certainties than ours.

The crockery: Initially the crockery is the crockery of the typical European house-proud housewife. As the play progresses it becomes obvious from the lines that the crockery, particularly in its "cracked" incorporation, is Nadia's "cunt." Thus the cracked crockery is representative of their failed marriage at the same time, and at a further remove the failed everything also. Thus, late in the play, when Nadia is deliberately breaking the crockery in front of the dirtied window through which she cannot even look to see the devastated park (note that it is the Jew who has been cleaning the windows to allow full vision), it is truly an upsetting act and moment.

The cock: Clearly a rooster, but the sexual connotation is un-avoidable. In one sense, our civilization's failure is perhaps too much "cock" and not enough "cunt," that is, too much machismo and all the cultural ramifications of it (e.g. war, weapons, competition, etc.), and not enough "cunt," crockery, and feeling. Note, for example, that when the judge wishes to get his wife into the bedroom he speaks of performing a quick "Anschluss," a "blitz-krieg," a "one-two-three boom-boom." Thus, the Jury's often contemptuous references to the cock. The Jew's "flucking," on the other hand, is quite a different thing, more culturally complex and ambiguous. There *is* something of a polarity in the play between justice-cock and crockery-cunt. I do not push all this too far, but I think it is there.

The Jew—Witness—Water Commissioner: Essential that he be a strong actor, lest the audience misunderstand (if only tempo-rarily) and see merely some unpleasant fun at the expense of the Jew. He is not the stock Jew but rather the Jew *playing* the stock Jew for his own deep reasons. He evades and frustrates the prosecutor's every feint and question. He *destroys* and *mocks* the courtroom procedure to follow his own ends. He recognizes that "justice" will not necessarily give him fair play. He must give back as much (and more) as he gets in this scene. *He* is the aggressor. He is also, it turns out, mysteriously involved with Nadia, the Judge's wife, and her children. Two of his survival masks are as window cleaner (see above) and milkman, i.e. he deals with *vision* and vital nourishment. It is to him that Nadia turns when she cannot bear her husband in his "robes." Indeed, as she puts it, "the milk man must be paid," i.e. essential life, reality, cannot be ignored or denied. Later, as the Water Commissioner, he tells us the truth straight out, first prettily, then harshly: e.g. it is all backing up, the pipes (of civilization) are clogged, nothing is clean but the shit itself, etc. At this point, even with a weak actor, there can be no doubt that this portrayal is no mockery of the Jew, but rather the Jew is making a hellish revelation of the cancerous state of society. His harsh squawks at his exit are a true underside of the cock's crow that ends the play.

Helmut: He is indeed the Judge, but not Klaus the law-giver, the man of "justice." Helmut is the executioner, the man who metes out "justice," the man who condemns. Just as the Jew reveals the underside of society, so Helmut reveals the underside of the Judge—the man who wears his robes to bed, the man whose children fear him, the man who always sleeps with a knife under his pillow. The conflict of civilization is also a conflict within him. But he does not until the end have any awareness of the Helmut in him. Nadia, however, does, and it is this schizophrenic living with *two* men that explains her predicament and her concern with the "cracked crockery." How can she make a life when the crockery is all cracked? As she puts it elsewhere: "There is too much in the closet." She cannot clean it out enough for them to make love as the Judge wishes. No amount of soup, sour cream, domestic bliss can truly cover over the "cancer." She is, thus, confused, all too human, angry, half-crazed, but also loving, vulnerable, and courageous, willing (even when all is lost) to renew, to go on.

The jury: Frequently anarchic and mocking, but essentially truth-telling. They *mean* lines like "We're with you, Jew." At a critical point in the play they cease "playing" and outrightly oppose and denounce the judge, thus provoking him to his final collapse into tragedy and knowledge. Essential that most of their lines be *heard*.

The brief vision of the bloodied and dead children: This can be expanded, if done very quickly, with slides of other destructions, e.g. the Jewish camps of World War II, post-Hiroshima victims, the tortures of totalitarian governments.

About The Author

KENNETH BERNARD lives with his wife and three children in New York City. He teaches at the Brooklyn Center of Long Island University. For his plays he has received Guggenheim, Rockefeller, and NY CAPS grants; for his fiction, NEA, NY CAPS, and NY Foundation for the Arts Grants; and for his poetry an Arvon Poetry Prize. His last book, *The Maldive Chronicles*, 1987, was a collection of short fiction. Early plays are collected in *Night Club and Other Plays*.